Stephen L. Newman

THE QUMRAN CAVE 12 MANUSCRIPT

D1475239

"Are existing religions merely a well conceived masquerade?"

ACKNOWLEDGMENTS

This book was created through the efforts of the editor, Paul C. Jeffers, and the input of my lovely wife, Charlotte.

TABLE OF CONTENTS

"Where there is invisibility, there is injustice."

—Mahatma Ghandi

Prologue

THE CREATION OF THE UNIVERSE

In the beginning, there was time, space, and energy concentrated into a single point—a primeval atom.

Approximately 14 billion years ago, a massive Presence entered our observable universe. The Presence created even further density, accented by unprecedented high temperatures. Seconds after the entry of the Presence, a cosmic inflation caused the universe to exponentially expand this primeval atom. George Lemaître, a Roman Catholic priest, coined the event "the Big Bang."

This Big Bang was not an explosion, but rather an expansion of space that led to the production of hydrogen along with traces of helium and lithium. Giant clouds of these elements coalesced through gravity to form 200 billion galaxies, each of which consisted of billions of stars.

The Big Bang is informally referred to as the birth of our universe, but more correctly, it merely represents a point in history where our universe entered into a state where the laws of modern physics work as we understand them.

The Presence also introduced the chemistry of life relatively early—somewhere between 10 and 17 million years after the birth of our universe.

Recent measurements of microwave background shifts in the supernova indicate that our universe is rapidly expanding. This expansion is, more likely than not, proof of the existence of a dark energy. There is simply not a sufficient amount of visible matter in our universe to explain the strength of gravitational forces amongst the myriad of galaxies.

Up to 90 percent of the matter in our universe is dark and does not emit light in any form. This matter is in the form of energy and represents the Presence that entered our universe 14 billion years ago.

The Presence has not decided if our universe is to reach a maximum size and then begin to collapse or if the expansion of the universe will only slow down and continue in perpetuity.

Who or what is this Presence?

Chapter 1

ZIPPAHAH

In the year 1103 BC, a small tribe of Pre-Essenes lived on the plains of Palestine. They were a monastic, female-driven order that, in part, practiced semi-pagan rites.

Zippahah led her tribe of thirty women and twenty men; she demanded that all members of the tribe maintain the highest possible standards of purity and holiness. Their love of virtue was proven by their freedom from money or high station. Their pleasure was found in temperance, having few wants, simplicity, a mild temper, lack of pride, and obedience to the law. All abided in these pleasures except for Samea, a male who often spoke of his apocalyptic art of telling the future.

Even in the face of her even temperament, Zippahah felt contempt for the fear that Samea placed in the vitality of her people.

Zippahah's tribe held no property and had a chronic fear of being contaminated by either social or sexual intercourse. Unpregnant women, without blood, joined with the males on Wednesdays for no other reason than to perpetuate the tribe;

there was neither love nor desire, only the need to reach an ascetic life and become worthy of being participants in the Holy Spirit.

Zippahah would deny Samea's entry into her tent on Wednesdays.

"You delight in intimidating my people; only my obedience to the Lord God prevents me from casting you from the tribe", she cried, "You will never have me!"

Samea would bow as he left Zippahah's tent but there was always a sinister half smile.

On a dreary winter night, the Lord God appeared before Zippahah and said,

"This is a divine revelation to be bestowed upon you only, Zippahah. Completion of the task that I am to ask of you will strengthen your desire to become a member of the Holy Spirit."

Zippahah was shaking uncontrollably and said to the Lord God, "I will do all that you wish."

The Lord God continued, "I will speak to you of my creation of the universe and all that exists. I ask you to record these revelations on copper plates, hoping that it can resist the ravages of time."

And so the Lord God spoke. Zippahah listened carefully and set down the words of the Lord God. That which was revealed by the Lord God was often obscure and mysterious. Fulfilling this task tired Zippahah, but the day came when the manuscript was finally completed.

The Lord God said to Zippahah of her achievement, "Zippahah, you have pleased me with your labors. Under any circumstances, hide the plates. Preserve them as you honor me in your heart. Finally, you must have the plates at your side at all times until I judge otherwise. Now, take rest, my Zippahah."

And then the Lord God disappeared.

The entire tribe had heard of the appearance of the Lord God and Zippahah's command by the Lord God to record the revelations. It caused great joy amongst the people. Samea was jealous and wished to discover the secrets of the plates.

On an early spring morning, Samea entered Zippahah's tent. With a deep bow he said, "The Lord God came to me last night and said there is to be lightning without rain and asked me to accompany you to the caves upon this occurrence, for he fears for your safety and the contents of the plates."

Reluctantly, and with suspicion, Zippahah replied, "Let me see this lightning without rain."

Days later, the lightning did come into the Palestinian plains, and the tribe ran deep into the caves just as several tents were afire, having been struck by this lightning without rain.

Samea closely followed Zippahah. In the chaos that ensued, Zippahah and Samea became separated from the other members of the tribe. A sense of dread struck Zippahah, but Samea looked to settle her and said, "Do not fear, I am familiar with these caves and soon we will rejoin the group."

It seemed to Zippahah that they were moving farther from the terrified screams of the tribe. Exhausted, Zippahah said, "I thirst."

"There is a small spring just ahead but be of care for it lies near a deep crevice," said Samea.

The small spring appeared and they knelt to drink. Quickly, Samea attempted to take the plates but Zippahah held the plates firmly to her breast. In the struggle, Zippahah stepped back and fell into the crevice. Zippahah knew she was going to die and would never enjoy the fruits of her Pre-Essenes tribe. For a mere moment, Zippahah saw her life. She had devoted her life to the Pre-Essenes, traded self-interests for those of her people, felt the loneliness of leading and the joy of serving, and now would never know any of these things again. Zippahah's calm eyes met Samea's rage as he made a final lunge to gain possession of the plates. He failed and Zippahah knew this. It was her last and final act of love for her people, for her Lord God, as she wrapped her body around the plates like a mother surrounds her child in a moment of danger.

Zippahah's body bounced off the sides of the crevice before she hit the bottom. In an attempt to conceal the plates and Zippahah's body, Samea threw stones and foliage into the crevice. With burning eyes he thought, *she got what she deserved!*

Neither Zippahah's body nor the plates were recovered.

Samea eventually became the leader of Zippahah's tribe and the mood of the Presence turned dark.

Chapter 2

SAMANTHA JAMES

Samantha James was a graduate from the University of Southern California with degrees in both archeology and biblical studies. She was the Dean of the School of Archeology at USC and also served as the Assistant Director of the Museum of Theological Studies in West Los Angeles.

Samantha was strikingly beautiful. Most of the students in her graduate archaeology classes were young men who were well aware of her lean and attractive figure. Typical of men their age, they would seize any opportunity to catch a glimpse of her cleavage or more exposed to view. She knew this gave her a certain power over men but she never abused it.

In addition to her beauty, Samantha was damn smart and everyone realized that she had an extraordinary capacity to feel sorrow for others' sufferings or misfortunes.

Her grandfather was a celebrated archeologist. Robert James was a senior advisor to Roland de Vaux in the excavation of the Qumran Caves. The Qumran Caves were located on the West Bank, approximately 1.6 kilometers north of the Dead Sea.

James and de Vaux discovered thirty fragments of the Dead Sea Scrolls in Cave 2. In Cave 4, they discovered remnants of the five scrolls that were torn into 15,000 pieces. Each of these discoveries were traced back to 300 BC through radiocarbon and paleographic dating.

Robert James, on occasion and under strict government observation, would take Samantha to the Qumran Caves. By the time she was fifteen, she had been to nine of the twelve discovered caves. Samantha loved the smell of soil mixed with antiquity.

In February of 2017, at the age of twenty-eight, Samantha accompanied University of Virginia researcher Dr. Oren Gutfeld to the cliffs west of Qumran. Their research led to the discovery of Cave 12. What was remarkable about the dig was, strangely enough, the absence of any scrolls.

Although they found only a small piece of an Aramaic manuscript rolled up in a jug, their findings clearly substantiated the fact that Cave 12 once contained scrolls that were later stolen as evidenced by the many pickaxes and empty scroll jars strewn throughout the surface of the dig.

According to the former chief editor of the Dead Sea Scrolls editorial team, John Stigner, there are at least six privately owned scrolls from Cave 12 that have not yet been made available for scholars. Among the missing scrolls, Stigner suggested, there may have been a complete Aramaic manuscript of the Book of Enoch.

Samantha often wondered why such scrolls were held in secrecy.

In 2022, Samantha received a call from Dr. Elezar el-Zebn, the Director of the Jordanian Department of Antiquities. In the most precise Queen's English, he said to Samantha,

"Dr. James, I have heard a great deal about you. For someone so young, you have acquired quite a reputation."

Samantha stammered, "Thank you, Dr. el-Zebn."

"We are going back into Cave 12," said El-Zebn. "A young Palestinian sheepherder was recently in 12 and found a small piece of pottery that holds an extraordinary piece of parchment. It has been traced to 1100 BC through both radiocarbon and paleographic testing. Even stranger is the text—it's not Hebrew, Aramaic, Greek, or Nalataean. It is in an ancient language with which we are not familiar. We think Cave 12 deserves another look and would like you to lead the dig."

Samantha was startled. "Why...why, yes, I would be honored."

"Excellent," replied el-Zebn. "I will arrange for your leave of absence from the University and I will have our private jet pick you up at LAX next Tuesday at 4:00 p.m.," he said with a sense of excitement.

"Yes sir, I'll be there!" Samantha replied, full of anticipation.

Samantha thought out loud, "1100 BC would push back the timeline of biblical manuscripts by at least a thousand years. Even if it's someone's delusion, it will give me a chance to get the hell out of L.A.!"

Chapter 3

QUMRAN CAVE 12

Of all the caves, Cave 12 had the most difficult entry. It was on a steep slope and was blanketed by dense shrubbery and huge boulders.

Samantha touched down in the West Bank four days before the arrival of her team. She was more than anxious to scope out the dig parameters.

Although she knew it was foolish, Samantha entered the cave at nightfall alone. She wanted to get a head start! Her curiosity was unconfined. She carried a large backpack with food, supplies, and lighting, just in case. She remembered the cave's interior and most of the meandering tunnels from her earlier visit.

Samantha decided to explore the northwest tunnel, for she and Gutfeld had spent very little time in this sector in 2017. The northwest tunnel was narrow and marked with numerous twists and turns. In 2017, they had discovered that this tunnel was barren of treasure.

It was 11:00 in the morning and Samantha wanted to be out of the cave by 2:00 p.m. She picked up her step in order to cover as much ground as possible. Suddenly, she took a quick turn and felt herself falling into a crevice. She felt her fingernails digging into the walls but the fall was inevitable. Her backpack helped break her fall, but she lost consciousness when she hit the bottom.

Samantha awoke amidst darkness hours later. She was a mass of bumps, scratches, and blood, but a quick inventory revealed only a broken leg and a severely sprained right arm. Possibly a concussion, but she felt as though she was coherent. The pain was excruciating.

She began to call out for help but realized this was absurd. She knew that there was no one here and blurted out loud, "There is no one here! I'm alone!"

The dig team wouldn't be there for three days. Samantha hoped her missed dinner with Dr. el-Zebn tomorrow night would raise sufficient suspicion.

Samantha found that one of her fluorescent lights had survived the fall. This would provide a moderate amount of incandescence for at least six hours. The flashlight attached to her hip would give an additional hour or two. She treasured these items, for she was frightened by dark, enclosed spaces.

Flashlight in hand, Samantha began to separate the remaining items in her backpack: a cell phone that was useless in the caves, traces of candy and power bars, a canteen, a jacket and—thank God—her reader. The pain in her arm and leg was inescapable, but with her reader, suffering could become optional.

She tried to get comfortable by elevating her broken leg and the badly bruised left arm. "Hydrate yourself!" she screamed. "The last thing you need to do is to go into shock." Samantha took a couple of bites of a shattered Hershey Bar.

Backing up against the wall, she saw skeletal remains with a right hand tightly gripping tarnished plates.

Samantha carefully removed the plates from the right hand and held her breath as she looked at them. There appeared to be seven small metallic plates in the form of a manuscript—maybe copper. Reaching for her cell phone, she was extremely careful not to cause damage to the metallic-like sheets. The review of the plates was the province of someone with a higher pay grade than her.

She thought, *Finally, I may have found something of archeological value and here I am in this goddamned hole in the ground.*

Samantha turned off the flashlight and fitfully slept on and off. She awoke in a burst of panic, screaming, "You had better hurry. My leg is swelling and I don't want to be a one-legged archeologist!" She slept again.

She had consumed all of her candy and had just a mouthful of water left. The last glimmer of the fluorescent light had faded yesterday. She was tired, cold, in the dark, and in pain.

In a dream-like state, Samantha thought she heard voices.

"I'm down here! I'm down here, goddammit, I'm down here!" she screamed.

Then Samantha heard el-Zebn's voice.

Chapter 4

QUITE A BIG DEAL

Samantha awoke in a Jerusalem hospital. IV's were everywhere. The constant beep of the heart monitor pounded in her ears, and she felt as though she was plastered with bandages. In a drug-induced haze, she was frightened by the lack of feeling in her left leg. The fear was allayed when she saw that the leg had been elevated. At least she hadn't lost it.

The attending physician, Dr. Stein, walked into her room. "You are a very lucky young lady. There was severe damage to the leg and I was afraid we were going to have to amputate," he said.

"Thank you, Dr. Stein," Samantha replied. "Is there anything else I should know?"

Dr. Stein replied, "You are going to limp for a while and may need a couple of visits to a plastic surgeon. It was a nasty fall, and you have a number of deep lacerations on your face and arms. I've closed them up, but as I said, you will need a plastic surgeon. Dr. el-Zebn and I both agree: you are too beautiful anyway—a few little scars will add character to your face," said Dr. Stein.

Samantha blushed and asked, "Where is Dr. el-Zebn?"

"He's right outside and is most anxious to speak with you," Dr. Stein replied.

Dr. el-Zebn then entered the room. He was thin, pale, and looked as though he hadn't slept in weeks.

"How are you, Samantha?" asked el-Zebn.

"Better, but I'm concerned about you," replied Samantha. "You look like you belong in this bed," she added.

"I am fine," said el-Zebn. "May I turn up the volume on your television?" asked el-Zebn.

What a strange request, she thought.

El-Zebn then turned the volume control to maximum. Dr. el-Zebn motioned to the TV as though referencing a scene playing out on the screen. His words did not match his carefree, happy smile as his head pivoted toward Samantha. "I don't want you to ask any questions or make any inquiries," said el-Zebn with emphasis. Quickly, he placed a small, newly designed microscopic chip known as a zip transfer under her pillow. "We are both in extreme danger!"

El-Zebn continued. "It is possible that we are under observation at this very moment. So please keep your voice down. You have been unconscious for nearly two weeks.

"In that time frame, an army of cryptographers and translators have been deciphering the manuscript in your copper plates. You and the plates have become quite a big deal. The armed forces have surrounded my laboratory and a litany of political and religious figures have been waddling in and out of our cryptography office. I have smuggled an abbreviated version of the manuscript and put it in the zip transfer under your pillow. I must warn you, though. You must never speak of this manuscript. I hesitated to even bring it to you.

"For all practical purposes, you were never in Cave 12 or discovered the plates. I feel that I must warn you again that you must not divulge even the slightest hint concerning this saga, including the contents of the zip transfer. If you do, we will rebut any accusations and claim you to be a heretic. There are those in the religious community who would consider taking your life," said el-Zebn.

"But, but..." Samantha stammered before el-Zebn interrupted.

"Please, no questions," said el-Zebn. "I must leave now. My absence will raise suspicions. As soon as possible, take leave of the hospital and return to the United States. By the way, prior to the flight they will search you and your luggage carefully. You know where to hide the vial.

I will tell those who are concerned that I told you the

contents of the plates were merely a precursor to the discovery of the Dead Sea Scrolls and were of little value. And by the way, they are destroying the copper manuscript.

I am not sure I will ever see you again. Godspeed, Samantha," said el-Zebn and he was out the door. Samantha never saw el-Zebn again.

Although Samantha was to take a private jet back to Los Angeles, el-Zebn was right. Security searched her belongings exhaustively and screened her body. They found nothing. Samantha, however, was sweating—she never sweat!

"Please, no cavity search," she prayed out loud. There was a discussion of such a cavity search, but with the large cast that extended from her foot to her hip, the thought was dismissed.

Samantha didn't relax until she was in the air and on the way home. Now all she had to do was recreate the details of the horrible motorcycle accident she had on the trip for the benefit of her friends and associates. Then, in the sanctity of her own private office, she could open the secret involving the "Big Deal."

Chapter 5

THE CAVE 12 MANUSCRIPT

W hen Samantha returned home, the California sun sliced through the blinds in her apartment. Manuevering her bags, crutch, purse, and keys to open the door of her two-bedroom apartment was akin to a bad juggling act. When she finally opened the door, she dropped her paraphernalia by the console table and hobbled to her couch. She turned on the light and sighed. The only photograph on the console was that of her grandfather on a dig. Tan, one knee up on a camp chair, it was as though he was staring at her. What would he do in her situation? He didn't answer. There was only silence.

Samantha was startled when she read of the fire in Dr. el-Zebn's lab. Dr. el-Zebn, his associates, and the cryptographic staff had all been consumed. No one survived. A chill crawled down Samantha's spine.

The next day, in the safety of her office, Samantha was frightened to open the zip transfer but could no longer resist the urge to see its contents. The transfer held a note from Dr. el-Zebn which read:

Dear Samantha,

The manuscript held in your plates was dated at approximately 1100 BC—one thousand years before the creation of the Dead Sea Scrolls. As you will see, it is an extraordinary discovery—perhaps too extraordinary!

The small disc has been translated into a modern English format but represents only 5% of the total manuscript. The disc cannot be copied and has a one-time shelf life. That is to say, after being played once, a chemical element in the disc will cause it to vaporize immediately. I have introduced the one time play feature for your protection. I am too old to fear for my life, but the existing circumstances foreshadow my early demise.

Your Friend, Elezar el-Zebn.

Samantha placed the disc in her computer and suddenly the translated version of the manuscript appeared:

In the beginning, the Lord God *created the heavens and earth. The earth was without form and was surrounded in darkness. The* Lord God *created light and She felt that this was good, so She separated the light from the darkness.*

The Lord God *created the earth and its plant and animal life over a period of six days.*

On the seventh day, She said, "Let us create a woman in my image." The Lord God *then formed woman from the dust of the ground and breathed into her nostrils. The woman then became a living being. The* Lord God *named the woman Eve. The* Lord God *then said, "It is not good for the woman to be alone. I will make her a helper to suit her needs."*

The Lord God *caused Eve to fall into a deep sleep and while she was sleeping, the* Lord God *created a man to be born of Eve's womb and then enclosed the place with flesh. Eve said, "This is man, born of my womb-flesh, and I shall call him Adam."*

The Lord God *had caused Eve to have more binah or intuition, understanding, and intelligence than the man. Eve was to keep the race alive and remain the goddess of the land and was to dominate the fish of the sea, the birds of the sky, and every animal that walked the earth. Eve was to have the power of the breadth of life. All living creatures would not exist without her.*

Adam, who was of Eve's womb, was stronger than Eve. He had but two purposes. The first was to provide seed to Eve who would, in turn, lead her to fill the earth. With his strength, Adam was also to assist Eve in perfecting her domain on earth.

The Lord God *blessed them and said, "Be fruitful and increase in numbers to fill the earth."*

Now the Lord God *planted a garden on earth that She called Eden. In the east of Eden, the* Lord God *planted all kinds of trees that were pleasing to the eye and good for food. In the middle of the garden was the Tree of Life. If Eve and Adam continued to eat from the Tree of Life, they would live forever.*

Adjacent to the Tree of Life was the Tree of Knowledge of Good and Evil. The Lord God *spoke to both Eve and Adam, "You are free to eat from any tree in the garden except for the Tree of Knowledge. If you are to eat from this tree, you will be in times of grief for all of perpetuity."*

The serpent was the craftiest of all animals that the Lord God *had made. While in the Tree of Knowledge, the serpent cornered Adam and convinced him to eat of the fruit from the Tree of Knowledge. Adam delighted in the taste of the fruit and felt empowered.*

Adam asked Eve to taste of the fruit but she refused, remembering the Lord God's *commandment. Wishing Eve to share in the pleasure of this fruit, Adam, with his overwhelming strength forced Eve to the ground and made her eat of the fruit. Eve delighted in the taste and asked for more.*

After they had consumed the forbidden fruit, the Lord God *appeared and asked Adam, "What is this that you have* done?" *Adam said, "The serpent deceived me and I ate the forbidden fruit and I forced Eve to share in my pleasure."*

The Lord God *now became aware of the fact that Eve and Adam knew of good and evil. She commanded that they were not to be allowed to reach out their hands to the Tree of Life, eat the fruit, and live forever. And so, the* Lord God *banned them from the Garden of Eden.*

The Lord God *was disillusioned by her living creatures and proclaimed...*

Suddenly, the transmission stopped and was followed by a message:

REMAINDER OF MANUSCRIPT DESTROYED OR UNINTELLIGIBLE.

Samantha stared intently at the screen, shaken by what it had revealed. She thought, "Perhaps they felt a female Lord God would rock civilization to its very core. Imagine if they realized my cell phone held photographs of the seven undeciphered copper plates. She remembered Dr. el-Zebn's warning. The warning only intensified her fears.

Chapter 6

STEPHEN JAMES

Stephen was a sergeant in the LAPD. After ten years on the force, he had become callous and beyond sensitive.

His attitude mirrored his beat, south central LA. He knew he was not as illustrious as his father—a discover of antiquities. But what could one expect? Stephen's life dealt with drug dealers, pimps, and whores, gang retaliations, murderers, and god-awful domestic disputes that, more often than not, ended in tragedy. Life for Stephen was just a short warm day between long nights.

Stephen was a tough cop. He never invited trouble but in dangerous situations he would recklessly push back.

He was accompanied in the squad car by his partner, Martinez. It was a typical late Saturday night call. The dispatcher, without emotion, stammered, "Robbery in progress at Enrico's Liquor Store…64th and Vermont…assailants appear to be armed and may be dangerous."

Martinez thought out loud, "What the hell does he know about dangerous while sitting in his comfortable chair? Martinez responded to the dispatcher, "we're on it—ETA five minutes."

Stephen slammed the gas pedal to the floor and turned on the siren. They came to a screeching stop in front of Enrico's, just as a potential suspect was running out the front door.

Martinez darted out of the squad car, screaming, "Stop! Put your hands on your head and turn around!"

The suspect spun around quickly, gun in hand. Martinez was quicker and put two bullets into the assailant's chest. He was dead before he hit the sidewalk.

Stephen carefully entered the liquor store. There was a quick movement behind the chip display.

"Drop your weapon and get down on the floor," Stephen exclaimed. "Do it right now, goddammit!"

There was no sound but a dark flash appeared at the end of the aisle. Instinctively, Stephen emptied his entire chamber.

As he approached a pool of blood, he stood in horror at the aisle's end. He had just killed an 8 to 10-year-old black child. The child was holding two Hershey bars.

"Oh my God, my God. I thought he had a gun," Stephen roared. Tears filled his eyes and he wept uncontrollably.

Stephen quit the force that night and shortly thereafter cashed in his 401K from his police profit sharing plan.

***

Four years later, Stephen James was ordained as an Episcopal priest. He was assigned to St. Paul's Cathedral in Los Angeles, just north of the USC campus. He became the leader of a congregation of blacks, Latinos, gays, lesbians, the homeless, and a variety of dogs and cats—just about anyone or anything that would attend his services.

As the son of a renowned archaeologist, and father of Samantha James, Stephen had turned to God. He knew, nevertheless, that he would not be able to erase the image of the black child in Enrico's.

The image persisted. Once while addressing his congregation, he cleared this throat while exploring the Gospel of Mark, when suddenly, he saw a flash from the third row.

Bam!! He was no longer in church.

Bam, Bam!! There he was in Enrico's liquor store, shooting a little boy who was in a pool of blood grasping two Hershey bars.

Stephen snapped back into the reality of the service, noticing that his spectacles had slid down in a river of sweat. He gripped the pulpit, steadied himself, and continued with the Gospel of Mark.

Nevertheless, the image continued to plague him. He knew he would never be able to forgive himself.

Chapter 7

ESCAPE

Once the computer disk was vaporized, a strange mist enveloped her office. Samantha composed a letter to her father, the only person in the world she could truly trust. Hurriedly, she threw her cell phone in her purse and made her way across campus.

As quickly as her leg cast would allow, she headed to the new Advanced Technical Studies building. She had an eerie feeling that she was being followed. It was one of those feelings that often send chills down one's spine.

She took the elevator to the third floor. She thought out loud, "I can't believe it—an elevator that actually works at USC." She exited the elevator and turned to Room 306. The nameplate was big and bold, just like its occupant, Winston Kelly, Associate Director of Neuromorphic Studies. Winston was a legend in his own mind, but he was damn smart and a loyal friend. Winston was actually in near love with Samantha, but he repeatedly lamented, "It's too bad I'm gay."

Samantha blew right past Winston's personal secretary and stormed into his office. Winston stared at Samantha and said, "You look like hell! Are you all right?"

"It was a motorcycle accident, but I'll be fine," said Samantha.

She leaned closer than usual to Winston and said, in a hushed tone, "Winston, I desperately need a couple of favors. These favors are to be between just the two of us. Any evidence of what we do today must be destroyed before I leave your office. Agreed?"

"Sure Sam, anything you want," replied Winston. "But these VIP services will cost you. You've got to introduce me to that new postgraduate assistant in your department. He's a doll."

Samantha was in no mood for Kelly's humor and cast a vile look towards him.

Kelly was taken aback. "This must be serious stuff. What's going on?" asked Kelly.

"Nothing I can tell you about," said Samantha. She pleaded, "Just do as I ask. Take my cell phone and transfer its contents to a zip. Make two copies."

Three hours later, she left Kelly's office and headed toward the faculty parking lot.

There was that eerie feeling again. Despite her leg, she attempted to halfway run to her car. She drove to her little apartment in the Hollywood Hills and noticed that Happy, her beloved basset hound, was not on the deck. Something was clearly not right!

Samantha heard Happy howling inside her apartment. She carefully opened the door to observe that the apartment was in a state of chaos. Papers were strewn everywhere. The file cabinets were pushed over, closets torn open. It appeared as though the apartment had been turned upside down.

That eerie feeling had now turned to real fear. She could feel the sweat collecting in her armpits. She remembered the sweat and the Tel Aviv airport and what an unpleasant sensation it was. "*Dammit, Samantha*, she said to herself, *you need a three-minute shower*. She despised the smell of body odor no matter the circumstances.

Instinctively, she grabbed a small suitcase, some clothing, her passport, cash she hid in a cleanser can under her kitchen sink, and Happy's leash.

She deposited Happy with her elderly next-door neighbor and hurried to her car. For no apparent reason, she looked under her car. Thank God there was nothing visible but oily grease spots.

As she opened her car door, the Band-Aid between her thumb and forefinger came off. There was no blood. She let the dressing fall to the garage floor. She took a fifteen-minute detour to the FedEx store at the bottom of the hill and then turned onto the San Diego Freeway towards LAX.

She parked in the long-term lot—the farthest from the airport. She waited an eternity for the tram. At long last, it finally arrived and dropped her off at the United Airlines terminal.

Samantha rushed to the international flight section and as she had done numerous times before, booked the 7:00 p.m. flight to Belize. To her left, she saw a tall blond man running through the airport, apparently looking for someone. She weaved through the crowds and headed towards the women's restroom, adjacent to the waiting area for the Belize flight.

A short while later, she casually left the restroom an hour later at 6:45 p.m. The tall blond man was nowhere in sight. Samantha boarded the flight. She called Bobby before takeoff.

Bobby picked up the phone and answered in his typical marijuana-high voice, "Heellooo."

"Bobby, it's Sam. I'm taking the 7:00 p.m. flight from LAX. Can you pick me up?" Samantha asked.

"Sure, Sis," said Bobby. "As always, I'll meet you right outside the waiting area."

Chapter 8

THE CATHOLIC CHURCH AND PETER MORRIS'S DESTINY

The Roman Catholic Church is, without question, the largest Christian church in the world. Approximately 1.2 billion people—or 18 percent of the world's population—has been baptized Catholic. As the world's oldest functioning institution, it has continued to play a prominent role in the development of Western civilization.

The leader of the Catholic Church is the Bishop of Rome, commonly referred to as the Pope. The totality of the legislative, executive, and judicial power of the Catholic Church rests with him. Above all, the Catholic Church teaches that it is the one true church, the universal sacrament of salvation for the human race, and the one true religion.

Peter Morris was a believer. Born of a Jewish father and a Catholic mother, his mother insisted he be raised Catholic. On his fourteenth birthday, Peter James Morris was baptized Catholic.

Peter and his family grew up on the east side of Philadelphia—the tough side. Peter was an optimist. He felt that there may have been more extraordinary places in the world other than Philadelphia, but he wondered if anything truly flourished in those other places.

After graduating from Syracuse, Peter joined the armed services. He became a member of the badassed special forces in the northwest Pakistan intervention. It was in the special forces that he learned indecision led to fear. He became decisive.

God's fifth commandment was, "Thou shall not kill." Peter had disregarded God's fifth commandment in Pakistan numerous times. He rationalized these acts by acknowledging that duty was a lofty consideration.

After the service, he did a one-eighty and entered the Catholic seminary. At twenty-eight he became a Catholic priest. He advanced through the church hierarchy with blazing speed. At thirty-five, Peter became a cardinal and was a powerful force in the College of Cardinals.

More importantly, Peter was a special pet of the 268th pope, Pope John. Peter, at 6 foot 3, 235 pounds, and with cropped blond hair, was often asked by Pope John to deal with sultry situations or those that required a special dispensation.

At 10:00 a.m. on Tuesday, Peter's direct line to Pope John rang. "Yes, Your Holiness? How can I be of assistance?" asked Peter.

The Pope replied, "Peter, I need your help. We have an issue that requires immediate and urgent attention."

"Of course, Your Holiness. I'll be in your office in fifteen minutes."

Peter arrived in the ornate offices of the Pope John, as promised.

"Please sit down, Peter. I will need your special skills," the Pope said solemnly. "A young archaeologist has purportedly discovered some metallic plates in a Qumran Cave that predate the Dead Sea Scrolls by more than a thousand years. A Jordanian professor and his staff of cryptographers apparently have deciphered the contents of the plates," the Pope explained.

Very calmly, the Pope continued, "These plates indicate that our Lord God is a female."

"That's preposterous!" said Peter.

The Pope continued, "Dr. Sumad, el-Zebn's closest associate, is one of my surveillants. He suggests that although several political and religious figures have been in and around el-Zebn's facility, only el-Zebn's staff is aware of the encrypted results. If these results were to become public, such an allegation, preposterous as it may seem, could immediately unravel the work of our Mother Church—a legacy that has evolved for nearly two thousand years.

"Make sure that the plates are completely destroyed and that el-Zebn and his associates are dealt with. We don't know if the young archaeologist is aware of the encrypted results. Find out and act accordingly. Later today, she will be released from an Israeli hospital and will be returning to the United States.

"You know what you have to do, Peter. You are my rock. Make haste—use my private jet and gather as much cash as you need from the safe. Godspeed, Peter," said the Pope.

Peter knew what he had to do. It was his duty.

Chapter 9

PETER MORRIS AT WORK

Peter had tied Dr. el-Zebn securely to an office chair. El-Zebn pleaded for mercy. He received none. Peter had learned a great deal in the special forces.

Peter thought, *It's strange how much torture this little man could endure.*

El-Zebn's body was a muddled blend of blood, tortuous burns, and knife carvings from the carnage inflicted on him.

In a dying gasp, el-Zebn whispered, "She knows nothing... nothing."

Either he was telling the truth or he was a brave little man, thought Peter. But he had to be absolutely sure. Peter set the timers for the incendiary explosives at five minutes. To cover his tracks, he slit the throat of the guard at the front door and quickly exited el-Zebn's laboratory. The remainder of guards patrolling el-Zebn's laboratory rushed to the blazing inferno.

Peter was off to the airport to interrogate the airport officials who had searched Samantha. He presented a counterfeit Israeli secret police badge to an airport security official and asked where the VIPs were searched.

The overweight official said, "Go to the second floor and look for the placard that reads 'Executive Search and Seizure.' Be careful, they are armed and sometimes they think they are playing cops and robbers."

"Oh, I'll be careful, officer," said Peter, as he felt for the .38 in his jacket pocket.

Peter found the office; it was locked. He slid his secret police identification under the door. A young man opened the door, apparently shaken by dealing with an agent of the secret police.

Peter stepped in with authority and said, "As you can see, my name is Jacob Brewer and I am the ISP agent assigned to document the search of the US citizen, Samantha James, earlier this afternoon."

The young man who answered the door said, "My name is Robert Hirsch." He extended his hand to Peter, expecting a handshake.

Peter didn't move. Then he asked, "Who conducted the search?"

Cautiously, Robert replied, "I did. I remember her distinctly.

She had a cast on her leg and was a real looker. She was about to board a private jet to Los Angeles. Despite the cuts and bruises, she was just gorgeous."

Peter snapped, "Tone down your testosterone, asshole. I'm not interested in her looks. I just want to know how you performed your search."

"We were instructed by Israeli police to conduct a careful search to ensure that she did not have in her possession any items that may be antiquities or any other unusual items. We examined every item in her luggage. A female officer did a body search and we scanned her. She was clean," Robert insisted.

"How do you know she was clean?" rebutted Peter. "If the police were concerned, you should have been concerned. Don't you think a cavity search should have been conducted?" said Peter raising his voice.

Robert responded, "We discussed a cavity search but it was impossible with the size of her cast."

"You fool, think about it. If she had to take a crap or a pee, you certainly could have had the opportunity to conduct a cavity search." Peter continued, red-faced. "Did you inspect her cell phone or computer devices?"

"No, she didn't have a computer. We didn't deal with her cell phone because of Israeli privacy laws."

"Privacy laws, my ass," said Peter. "You're an idiot!"

Peter was still unsure. He left immediately for LA on the Pope's private jet.

After arriving in LA, Peter went directly to Samantha's apartment. He was searching for something, anything. He found nothing.

After a number of near-miss encounters, he thought he had traced Samantha to the United Airlines terminal. She melded in with the crowds and he lost her. He thought aloud, "Peter, you're losing your edge."

Chapter 10

DEAR DADDY

Samantha loved her father dearly. With the death of her mother at Bobby's birth, they had developed a special connection. Her father was the only person in the world that she could really trust. Despite an inner sadness, he was willfully strong and a man of conviction.

Stephen James was in his private office in the back of St. Paul's Cathedral. He was preparing his sermon for next Sunday's service when he heard a loud voice.

"Hello, is anyone here?" It was the FedEx courier. He paused, "I am looking for the Right Reverend Stephen James."

"I am Reverend James," said Stephen.

The courier handed him a package and asked for Stephen's signature.

Walking back to his office, he opened the package to find a letter from Samantha along with a very small electronic component enclosed in a sturdy ring box. The letter appeared to have been hastily handwritten:

Dear Daddy:

You know I love you more than anything in the world. I need a favor. I need you to hide this newly designed zip transfer from my cell phone. It is extremely valuable and confidential. It may fit in one of the chambers of your .38 revolver at the cathedral. I didn't want to meet you at St. Paul's. I'm a dreadful mess after a fall at a Qumran Cave. My appearance would only cause you concern.

Don't worry, I'm alright. I just need a little time to mend.

I found something at the Qumran Cave 12 dig. It could possibly change all of our lives. This is the reason for the zip transfer. I think I am being followed and I am going into a mole-mode until I can sort all of this out.

You have taught me to take care of myself, but I'm sure I'll need you eventually.

Love you Always, Sam

Stephen was confused, angry, and concerned.

But as she says, Stephen thought to himself, *I did raise her to take care of herself.* Nevertheless, if he found that anyone was to lay a hand on her, there would be more than hell to pay.

Chapter 11

ROBERT JAMES

Robert James Jr. was named after his grandfather, the celebrated archaeologist who was instrumental in the discovery of the Dead Sea Scrolls.

His sister, Samantha, was the star. In high school she garnered straight A's, was student body president and the captain of the championship girls' volleyball team. Then there were the academic scholarships to USC and dual degrees in archaeology and biblical studies.

Bobby was an atheist and never knew the reason for the degree in biblical studies. Nevertheless, Bobby often wondered if Samantha could do anything wrong.

Bobby was the gentle, distant one who had a bit of playful mischief about him. He knew he could never catch up with Sam, but who could?

Bobby distinguished himself in high school by handcuffing Samantha's boyfriend to the chain-link fence abutting the football field. Of course, Samantha would say he was drop-dead gorgeous, captain of the football team, and on his way to Harvard.

The vice-principal, Mr. Johnson, saw no humor in Bobby's exploit and demanded that Bobby give him the key to the lock.

Bobby was expressionless and said, "I guess I lost it."

A janitor had to be called to extricate the captain of the football team. Samantha laughed her ass off.

Bobby spent three days in detention, but he didn't care.

At a very early age, Bobby realized that Samantha was his father's favorite. It was easy to explain, he thought. She was just plain better at everything. Beyond Samantha, there was always the fact his mother died bearing Bobby. Bobby blamed himself for her death and he often thought that his father felt the same.

An irreparable rift had developed between Bobby and his father. The gap was never bridged and at eighteen he joined the Marine Corps. No "goodbyes" were said.

Bobby spent seven years at Camp Pendleton and found a home in the Corps. He had distinguished himself in hand-to-hand combat and tactical arms. Eventually, he became a sergeant commanding a small unit in the exclusive CRD (Clandestine Reserve Division).

On February 3, he was ordered to an in-and-out mission in northern Pakistan. His commander was insistent:

"Cross the border, create some rudimentary maps, take a

bunch of photographs, and get out before the Pakistani rebels blow your heads off!"

After crossing the Pakistan border, three clicks to the north, Bobby heard gunfire.

"It isn't our job, but I just want to be sure that none of our guys are left in this damned place. Let's go, girls!" cried Bobby.

Bobby had become his father; he didn't invite trouble, but in dangerous situations he would recklessly push back.

Bobby could see that the Pakistani rebels held the high ground and were slaughtering an army infantry unit below them.

"Robinson, Parker, Williams, and Jensen, go assist the Army pansies. Jules and Villa, you come with me. We'll try to flank them," said Bobby in a hushed tone.

As Bobby crawled up the side of the small hill, he turned back to see that three of the four sent to assist the Army unit were blasted by a mortar shell. Legs and arms were tossed into the air.

One Marine was screaming in anguish, "Help, help me! I've been hit!"

An Army infantry officer heard the cries and tried to reach him. Pakistani bullets riddled his body before he was able to reach the ailing Marine.

Bobby whispered, "Now I'm really pissed."

Approaching the ridge from behind, Bobby motioned to Jules and Villa to lob their grenades into the Pakistani stronghold. The three grenades appeared to have done their job. Without warning, however, a remaining rebel took out Jules and hit Bobby knocking him to the ground. Villa covered Bobby with his own body and emptied his chamber into the Pakistani's contorted body.

Villa quickly inserted another clip and screamed, "Damn you! Damn you! Damn you!

Then there was silence.

Bobby awoke in the hospital. A man was standing above him. The tall stranger, a member of the Army Special Forces, said to him, "Sergeant James, I'm heading back to the States. I wanted to stop by and thank you, personally, for saving me and the lives of my men. We lost half of my unit but, without you, we would all be dead! You have a great deal of courage. I understand you and Villa have been nominated for the Medal of Honor. It's well deserved."

Bobby was reeling in and out of consciousness with the amount of drugs pumping through his body. He had lost his right arm and most of his right shoulder. The pain was excruciating and he wondered if it would ever stop. Strange as it seems, the pain was localized in his right arm—the arm that had been removed.

The tall soldier bent over and said, "If you're ever in Philadelphia, look me up and we'll get drunk together and tell each other lies. My name is Morris—Peter Morris."

Chapter 12

BELIZE

Belize is a small country located on the eastern coast of Central America. Its population is just shy of 400 thousand and it has an area of approximately 8,800 square miles.

Bobby's closest friend in the Corps, Enrique Villa, was born and raised in Belize. Villa often teased Bobby with tales of a Caribbean lifestyle, the lovely, half-clothed Latin girls, and the ability to earn lots of money, fast.

Belize allows non-residents to establish offshore accounts. This, along with the fact that the Belize dollar is pegged to the US dollar, allows drug traffickers and money launderers to flourish. Villa's brother, Ernesto, was the largest trafficker in Belize.

After his medical discharge from the Corps, Bobby called Villa, asking him if he could bunk down at his place in Belize until he could get settled in.

"Sure, Bobby, anything you want," said Villa.

Villa picked him up in a new, black Mercedes at the airport

and drove him through the forested countryside to a gated home. The home was surrounded by armed guards. As they entered the compound, Bobby came to realize that this was not a home—it was a palace, accommodated by fine artwork, furniture, fountains, and servants at every corner. Most of the servants were native women of Belize who were exquisitely beautiful with large breasts. Bobby tried not to stare.

Ernesto arrived in the living room, adorned in a beautiful white suit with a plumeria flower in his buttonhole.

"Welcome to my home," said Ernesto. "Enrique thinks a great deal of you and feels that even with one arm, you can handle a weapon better than anyone he has ever seen. Is this true?"

Sheepishly, Bobby retorted, "I seem to have a knack in dealing with weapons, even one-handed."

Enrique was at his side when Ernesto made a proposal, "I would like you to work with my brother. It's not much, but special situations sometimes arise. I will pay you ten thousand American dollars per month. This should provide you with more than enough to buy a little home in Belize City and meet most of your needs. In return, all I ask of you is your loyalty. Any violation of our loyalty pact and you will beg for death. Do you understand?"

Enrique was on his heels swaying back and forth and looking uncomfortably at the marble floor.

"Yes, sir, I understand," said Bobby.

"Excellent," said Ernesto and pulled a stack of hundreds out of his pocket. Quickly, Ernesto added, "Now go buy some new clothes that don't smell of marijuana."

As they walked out, Bobby said, "For ten thousand dollars per month, the special situations must be very special."

Enrique said nothing.

Bobby enthusiastically called Sam to tell her he was in Belize City and to come down as soon as she could. There was no call to his father. They could never reconcile—they were too much alike.

***

In the beginning, the jobs assigned to Bobby were cursory. Counting cash, distributing cash to Parliament members, police officials and, most importantly, to Father Colville, the leader of the Roman Catholic Church in Belize City. Ernesto donated $25,000 per week to the Catholic Church, principally to feed the starving mestizo and Creole children.

When the September celebrations were to begin, Ernesto summoned Bobby and Enrique to his home.

"Father Colville has received a communication from the office of Pope John," he said. "His Holiness wishes to deal with Ricardo Corales.

"Corales is a known atheist and Communist. It appears that the number of his supporters continues to grow. With this growth, the attendance at Father Colville's last church continues to decline along with the contents in the weekly collection plate.

"Corales is planning an armed demonstration during the course of our September festivities. The demonstration is to end symbolically at the steps of Father Colville's church. His Holiness asks that Corales be dealt with locally and with the utmost of confidentiality," Ernesto explained. Looking at Enrique and Bobby, Ernesto asked, "Do you understand me?"

As they walked out of Ernesto's home, Bobby was uncomfortable. "Is the Pope asking us to assassinate Corales?" he asked.

"Yes," said Enrique, "and we are going to do it! Remember, Bobby, you owe me!"

Ricardo Corales lived in a small home just outside of Belize City. Hooded, Enrique and Bobby tried the back door. It was locked. They heard male laughter and the clanking of glasses.

They had no choice; they broke through the door and confronted two men at a card table. Corales was not one of them.

Enrique yelled, "Put your hands on the table—anyone that moves will be quickly sent to hell. Where is Corales?" Enrique demanded.

Corales suddenly burst out of the bathroom, grabbed Enrique by the neck, and planted his gun firmly on Enrique's temple. Enrique dropped his gun. Looking at Bobby, Corales said, "Drop your gun or your friend will soon be sleeping with the fish."

Instinctively, Bobby raised his gun and in a millisecond blew off Corales's face. The bullet creased Enrique's skull. Blood poured from his hairline. Bobby then turned to the two men at the table and at point-blank range killed both of them.

Enrique turned to Bobby and said, "You could have killed me."

"Enrique," said Bobby, "consider the alternative. I could have killed you but Corales most certainly would have killed you."

As they dropped the bodies off the back of a boat, the shark-infested waters erupted in blood.

Bobby turned to Enrique and said, "I QUIT! Now we're even." Bobby had to trust Enrique to make it right with Ernesto.

Bobby purchased a 28-foot sport fishing vessel and quickly became a popular captain. His killing days were over.

Chapter 13

ARRIVAL

Bobby was sitting in the waiting area when Samantha appeared. She was bruised and had a cast on her leg.

Before Bobby could open his mouth, Samantha said "Shut up, Bobby, I don't want to talk about it. I had a motorcycle accident."

Bobby, with his devilish attitude, couldn't resist getting in the last word. "Afterwards, did you beat the crap out of the bike?"

Samantha stood there, but then punched Bobby in his good arm with a smile.

"Ow!" Bobby wailed. "Beating up a disabled veteran, a decorated one, by the way, does not fit your compassionate image," said Bobby.

Samantha retorted, "Right now, I don't feel like my compassionate self." They then headed to the parking lot.

Bobby stopped in front of a new Jeep Ranger and said, "What do you think?"

Samantha said, "No way! Did you win the lottery?"

"Made a little money when I first arrived and now the sport fishing boat is in the black. I can't complain", said Bobby.

"I am trying to remember when I have ever heard you complain," said Samantha. She patted him on the shoulder. The good one.

After several glasses of wine that night, Samantha opened up a little to Bobby.

"Bobby," she said, "I've got some trouble. It involves my recent dig in the Qumran Caves. I found something that may be extremely valuable but it's equally as dangerous."

With an acrid tone, Bobby said, "Don't tell me, you found the body of Jesus Christ encased in an ancient UFO."

"Quit screwing around, Bobby. I don't need a dose of your non-stop atheism. This is really serious," stressed Samantha. She began to cry.

Bobby knew he had gone too far. He couldn't remember Samantha ever crying. "What is it, Sam? What can I do to help," he asked.

"Just stay close to me—real close," Sam sobbed.

***

Bobby picked up his cellphone in the morning and saw a number on-screen that was unfamiliar. He noticed there was a voicemail:

Mr. James: This is Peter Morris in Philadelphia. You once saved the lives of several of my men in Pakistan. No small matter, but you also saved my life. I have been looking all over for you and came across your name in a fishing magazine. I would love to see you again, and perhaps you could haul me out to the Belize barrier reef, where I might be able to hook into a large blue or black marlin.

Bobby couldn't remember placing an ad in a state side magazine. Perhaps it was just a testimonial from a satisfied customer.

Bobby sent a text to Morris:

Mr. Morris: Would love to see you. I think I'm in better shape than the first time we met. Perhaps we can sit down, have a couple of drinks, and tell each other lies. But first of all, let's go fishing. I'll provide all of the equipment and lunch. How about Thursday or Friday of next week? I'm in the Canary docks just outside of Belize City. My boat is called Choggy's Red. Call me. -Bobby.

Seconds later, Morris texted back:

Bobby I'll meet you at Choggy's Red at sunrise next Thursday. Looking forward to some great fishing. Call me.

Peter

Strange, thought Bobby. Maybe he's just a rich American—he didn't even ask about the charter price.

Chapter 14

SAMANTHA AND PETER

O ver the next seven days, Samantha stuck like glue to Bobby. She followed him everywhere—she even served as the mate on the charter boat despite a chronic case of seasickness.

Samantha had put the Qumran Cave, the death of el-Zebn, and her escape from LA in a place that boiled in her head but no longer elicited terror.

At sunrise on Thursday, Bobby and Samantha fired up the twin screwed engines, dressed the poles, selected favorite lures, drug out the teaser, and extended the cover for soon to be required shade. They waited for Peter Morris.

Shortly after 5:15 a.m., Peter was on the dock. He caught sight of Bobby and ran to the ship, Choggy's Red. Peter jumped aboard and hugged Bobby. Bobby didn't expect a hug from a bear of a man!

Bobby thought, *I don't care if he is gay—just as long as he pays the freight.*

"Good to see you again," said Peter. "You're right—you do look much better than the last time I saw you."

"You have caught me at a disadvantage. I remembered very little while in the hospital. Nevertheless, it's a pleasure to meet you, at least while I am in a lucid moment."

Eyeing Samantha, Peter said, "And who is this magnificent creature?"

"This is my sis, Samantha. Most of us call her Sam," said Bobby.

Peter took Samantha's hand and commented, "If you don't mind, I will call you Samantha. Samantha is regal and mirrors your beautiful face."

Samantha squeezed Peter's hand. She realized her mouth was open, but quickly pretended she was just biting her lip.

They had fallen in love at first sight, with a touch of lust.

My God, she thought. *This guy is dirty handsome: tall and blond—something like a Grecian God.* Suddenly, she flashed back and a sense of dread struck her. She caught herself and thought quietly, *No, it can't be—it would be an immense leap.*

"Let's go fishing," Bobby said. Peter agreed.

They headed to sea and shortly after reaching the reef, Bobby shouted, "Fish on!"

Peter grabbed the pole, set the hook, and within an hour proceeded to bring in a 200-pound striped marlin.

Peter was half-hearted in his desire to keep fishing. He couldn't keep his eyes off of Samantha. Samantha glared back.

"What do you do for a living, Peter?" asked Samantha.

"Nothing very special," Peter said. "I buy and sell religious antiquities. It's all quite boring, but if you like I would be happy to continue to bore you over dinner at the Marriott. Say, 7:30 p.m.?"

Samantha said, "That's great! I'm an archaeologist and I can bore you with tales of digging in the dirt."

Bobby turned back to home. No one seemed to be interested in continuing the fishing adventure. As Peter exited the boat, Bobby noticed he was carrying. As Peter left the dock, Bobby alerted Samantha that Peter had a weapon.

"Stop it, Bobby," she said. "This is Belize and half of the population carries guns."

***

After dinner, Samantha and Peter went up to his suite in the Marriott. They made mad, passionate love over and over and over again despite the cast on her leg. She had never met a man like this. But…

Over the course of the next two weeks, they spent every waking moment together. He would entertain her with tales of his world travels, sometimes adding nuances in French, Italian, and Spanish—all languages that he commanded.

Samantha told him about her grandfather and the Dead Sea Scrolls, about digs and Qumran Caves and other places that were hotter than the sun. Peter seemed to be very interested.

Peter knew it was wrong, but he couldn't see Samantha sitting in a chair much like el-Zebn had done. Peter loved Samantha, but it conflicted with his sense of duty. Perhaps there was an alternative.

Two weeks after they met, Peter proposed. An emptiness had suddenly been filled, an emptiness he didn't even know he had.

Samantha wept when she said, "Peter I can't marry you. I can't marry anyone. If you were to marry me it would be your death sentence."

"I don't scare easily. Let me help," said Peter.

"You can't help," she replied back.

Peter caressed Samantha in his loving arms and said, "Oh yes, I believe I can help you."

Samantha knew she was approaching a cathartic breakdown. Finally, she crumbled.

"All right, all right," she cried. "I found something in a Qumran Cave dig. They were some form of metal plates and predated the Dead Sea Scrolls by over a thousand years. I had taken pictures of the plates on my cell phone and forgot about them."

Samantha suddenly sensed that fear and became, for some unknown reason, less than genuine.

She continued, "A Jordanian archaeologist apparently deciphered the contents of the plates. He told me they were merely precursors to the Dead Sea Scrolls. But when I read of the Jordanian's violent death, I became suspicious and then terribly frightened.

"I had the pictures of the plates removed from my cell phone and relayed them to an electronic device that could not be duplicated—a zip transfer. Since then, I have been running."

"For your safety, where did you hide this zip transfer?" Peter asked.

"You must not tell anyone this," she demanded. "My father holds the transfer, probably in St. Paul's Cathedral in LA. My father is an Episcopal priest and is the only man who I can really trust." Sam didn't tell Peter of the duplicate zip transfer embedded in her palm.

"You can trust me," Peter assured her.

Samantha awoke in the king-sized bed in the Marriott suite. She called, "Peter, Peter, where are you?" Peter didn't answer.

Samantha saw an envelope on the dresser and rushed to open it. It read:

Dear Samantha,

I love you more than anything in the world but you won't see me again. You and Bobby may be engaged in a dramatic piece of history. However, your lives in this chronicle are inconsequential and can be taken at any time. I have left approximately $250,000 in the bottom drawer. Use this to survive. I have also arranged a private plane for you at the Belize airport. It will take you wherever you wish.

You will read in the newspapers about the violent explosion on Choggy's Red. Apparently there were two on the ship when it sank. The flames and sharks exacted their toll— not even dental records were an option to provide a discerning ID. This incident will reveal the volatility of your current circumstances.

I needed something tangible to remember you by, so I have taken the ring off your pinky. You must do as I say immediately and tell no one of your situation!

I will always love you,

Peter

More frightened than confused, Samantha dragged Bobby from his little home in a big sister fashion.

"Grab some essentials, especially cash," she said with a great sense of urgency. "We're getting out of here now!"

Bobby was howling, "But Sam, where, what…"

Samantha put an end to his pleas, shouting, "Shut up and follow me if you want to live."

Chapter 15

THE RETURN TO ROME

Peter decided to wear his vestments to the meeting with Samantha's father. It wasn't to impress; it was to express the gravity of the circumstances.

Stephen James was alone in the Cathedral, admiring the sun's reflections on the near-ancient church windows when Peter arrived.

Peter approached Stephen James and introduced himself to the Reverend James. "My name is Father Morris. I am a special aid to his Holiness, Pope John. I am going to give you some very important information about Samantha and Bobby."

"Are they all right?" asked Peter.

"Yes, they are currently safe, but this could change dramatically based upon the results of our discussion," stated Father Morris.

"Are you threatening me?" asked Stephen.

"Quite to the contrary, I am trying to save their lives," said

Father Morris. "We can agree on a course of action and they will live. If we cannot agree, I can assure you that your children will be dead within six months.

"Your daughter has discovered a rather significant piece of religious history. Unfortunately, the repercussions of such a discovery could literally turn the world upside down. Samantha has told me that you hold an electronic device—a zip transfer in your possession. You must surrender this device immediately," stressed Peter.

"How can I possibly believe you when my children are nothing more than pawns?" Stephen asked.

Peter said, "Believe as you will, but I love your daughter and was prepared to depart Mother Church for her. Even with my departure, she would still be in constant jeopardy. The only way to save Samantha and Bobby's lives is to destroy the zip transfer."

Peter offered Stephen Samantha's ring and said, "I have this ring as a tangible memory of our love." Peter had no intention of surrendering this keepsake.

"Follow me into my private office," said Stephen.

Stephen opened the top drawer of his desk and pulled out a 38. Peter didn't move.

"My life is worth nothing to me. I only care about Samantha's survival," Peter said.

Stephen opened the chamber and handed the zip transfer to Peter.

***

Peter entered the Pope's private quarters with trepidation. He knew that he was destined to deceive the leader of the Catholic Church.

"Well, Peter, have you solved our problem?" asked the Pope. "Our pilot suggested he had taken you to Belize. It was unfortunate to read of the death of a man and woman two days ago from the very same location. Was this your work?"

"Yes, Your Holiness," replied Peter. "The young archaeologist and her brother had to be dealt with. The archaeologist had photographed the Qumran plates and transferred them to a newly designed zip transfer. I don't think she knew of the contents of the plates, but someone else could have deciphered them. For our safety, I destroyed the zip transfer."

The Pope turned to Peter and said, "Thank you, Peter. You are my rock."

"Sit down, Peter," said the Pope. "We have another situation in Brazil that will require your attention."

Chapter 16

THE BAR SB RANCH

Stephen James, as a cop in the Los Angeles Police Department, had often seen people disappear. He once told Samantha, "If you ever need to vanish, there are two places you can go. Belize is one, the other is the state of Oklahoma. In either place, it's possible to dissolve into a state of almost non-existence."

Samantha and Peter had exhausted the Belize alternative. They exited the plane on an airstrip outside of Tulsa, Oklahoma. Their belongings were meager—the clothes they wore, a small cosmetic case, a suitcase holding over $350,000 in cash, and two .38's. The Uber driver drove them into Tulsa proper.

Bobby abruptly told the Uber driver to stop. Sam was confused.

They were in front on the Choctaw Used Car Lot. The signage read, "Reliable Cars at Honest Prices." Bobby paid the driver and headed directly to a black 2015 Ford F-250. It clearly needed a paint job and bodywork. But neither he nor Samantha cared. They just wanted something that was functional and unobtrusive.

Bobby asked the salesman how the truck ran. The salesman responded, "Just like it came off the showroom floor. Only sixty-five thousand on the engine. Take it for a spin."

Bobby took the keys and was gone for nearly a half an hour. Samantha was nervous.

Bobby turned into the driveway, opened the truck door, faced the salesman and asked, "How much?"

The salesman said, "It's a steal at $9,000."

"Well so much for the honest pricing," he thought to himself. "I'll give you eight. It needs a couple of pistons, a new carburetor, and a valve job," Bobby replied.

The salesman said, "How about $8,500?"

Bobby was a reverse negotiator. "Now my offer is $7,500."

The somewhat stunned salesman said, "Ok, ok. A deal at $8,000."

Bobby and Samantha drove out of the lot like modern-day characters out of the novel entitled *The Grapes of Wrath*. That's what they wanted, at least for now.

They drove for hours into southwestern Oklahoma. The drive was lulling, for it was an endless landscape of short grass prairies and an occasional white-tailed deer or American bison.

They drove through to Wilkinson, Oklahoma. The welcome sign read, "The Home of The Oklahoma Prairie Chicken, Population 8692."

Ten miles outside of town, they saw a sign that read, For Sale: 260 Acre Wheat Farm and Cattle Ranch."

Samantha said, "Turn in."

Bobby quickly replied "Samantha, we don't know a goddamned thing about cattle ranching or wheat farming. What the hell are you thinking?"

"After what I've told you, you should realize I'm thinking about keeping us alive," Samantha responded.

They met the owner, Lucas, at the front door. Lucas said, "Howdy, folks, what can I do for you?"

Samantha said, "We noticed your 'For Sale' sign out front."

"Ok then, come on in," said Lucas. "I never talk business without a cup of coffee in my hand," he added.

Lucas looked them over and said in a straightforward, honest fashion, "I don't mean to be critical, but you folks just don't look much like farmers or ranchers."

"We aren't," said Samantha, "but we're hardworking and quick studies."

Lucas was also a quick study and could read into people's souls by gazing into their eyes. He saw fear in the eyes of Samantha and Bobby.

"If you're running from something," continued Lucas. "It's none of my business, but here's my offer: $250,000 for the farm and inventory—one-half down and $1,000 per month at 3% until the note is paid off. You'll also have to keep old Elias as a farm hand. He's a good worker and doesn't have any other place to go. You'll have to pay him $850 per month and give him three squares," he added.

Samantha responded without consulting Bobby, "Sounds like a fair deal to us. Let's get an attorney to draft the contract."

Lucas looked sternly at Samantha and said, "Don't need no attorney—don't trust 'em. I'll give you the deed. I can tell you won't cheat me—even if you did, you know I have lots of land and a shovel. They would never find you."

Neither Bobby nor Samantha felt threatened.

"Might as well tell you," said Lucas. "Our neighbor is a strange one. He looks like a city fella and has only said hello to me once in three years. Looks like he's hiding but it ain't no mind to me."

"One last thing," Samantha interjected, "we saw several large homes as we left town and in the driveway each had a very expensive car like a Ferrari or a Maserati and then a beat up old pickup truck. Seems strange."

Lucas responded immediately, "It's the oil. The old man needs a work truck and the wife, young or old, wants a fancy car. Never cared much for oil or its trappings."

Within an hour, Lucas had gathered a few personal belongings and was out the door. They never saw Lucas again.

Samantha fell in love with the ranch-prairie grass, twenty head of cattle, two horses, and a small but cozy home. The back of the property was abutted by a sky island mountain range.

"Shall we call it the Bar SB Ranch?" asked Samantha.

"Why are you always first?" replied Bobby.

Samantha smacked Bobby in his good arm. "Don't be an idiot! Then we would have to call it the Bar BS Ranch," Samantha said laughingly.

Suddenly, Samantha felt an unfamiliar cramp.

Chapter 17

BRAZIL

Peter flew into the Brazilian airport and headed directly to Saint Mary's Catholic Church. He was dressed in the full garb of a senior Catholic priest. Father Esteban met him at the church entrance.

"Father Esteban," said Peter. "It is a pleasure to meet you. My name is Peter Morris and I am a special aid to our beloved Holiness, Pope John."

Father Esteban was caught off guard by the presence of one so close to Pope John. He said, "Why…why it's a pleasure to meet you, Father. We have an unsettling issue involving one of my parishioners, Maria Luiz. The local newspapers have published her story and it has resulted in a terrible controversy."

Peter arrived at Maria's small farm after a two-hour drive. Chickens and pigs were wandering aimlessly about the property.

Maria had three small children. Her husband Rodriguez was tending to the fruit trees.

As he examined the farm and home, he wondered how

they could survive in this wilderness. *God has mercy on the poor,* Peter thought to himself.

Peter went to the door and softly knocked.

Maria opened the door with caution and put her finger to her lips: "Shhhsh, Father," she said. "My little ones are napping."

Peter spoke in a guttural Spanish dialect, "I apologize, Mrs. Luiz. My name is Peter Morris and I serve our Holiness, Pope John."

"Oh, my Lord!" she exclaimed. "Directly from the Pope? My heart is beating like the bells of St. Mary."

"Relax, Mrs. Luiz," said Peter. "The Pope is very interested in you but would like you to answer a few simple questions," said Peter.

"Whatever his Holiness desires," said Maria.

"Maria, you told Father Esteban that our Lord God appeared before you. Is that correct?" asked Peter.

"Oh, yes. She appeared before me, just before dusk in the fields. She asked that I continue to spread the word of Her existence," said Maria.

"Pardon me, Maria, but you must have been in the midst of a dream or in a very anxious state," said Peter.

"Oh no, Father. I was returning home from the fields. I was alone, for Rodriguez had already returned home to gather the children. She was most gentle and comforting. I was very proud that She chose to speak to me. She promised that She would visit me again to speak of things that are to come," insisted Maria.

Peter responded, "I am sorry, but you must understand you might have been visited by our beloved Virgin Mary, but certainly not by our Lord God."

"Oh yes, Father. She told me She was our Lord God. I was confused so I ran immediately to meet with Father Esteban. He said the same as you are telling me now that I was visited, perhaps, by the Virgin Mary. That is not true! She said She was the one and only Lord God," Maria insisted.

"Maria, I want you to dispel of any notion of a woman Lord God. It can only be the work of the devil," said Peter.

"But Father Peter, I swear!" Maria held firm.

Maria couldn't continue, for Peter had rushed into the children's room and lined them up closely in front of her face.

Peter put a gun to the smallest child's head. Maria covered her mouth in terror and began to cry.

"Once again, Peter stated, "I must tell you Mrs. Luiz, you may have seen the Virgin Mary, but not our Lord God. I want you to recant this nonsense. I need you to confess your sin to Father Esteban at tomorrow's service. If you do not absolve yourself of this sin, each of your children will be murdered. Do you understand me?" said Peter forcefully.

"Oh yes, I understand you," Maria said. "What was I thinking? I made a terrible mistake; it must have been the Virgin Mary. Please don't hurt my babies," she pleaded.

After Maria's confession the next morning, Peter gathered Maria, her husband, and the three children and led them to the Pope's private jet. He dropped the family off in a small village two thousand miles south of the Brazilian capital and gave them $5,000 American dollars.

Maria hoped she would never hear from the church again.

This would be his Peter's second lie to the Pope. First, he had lied about destroying Samantha's zip transfer and now he was going to lie about his dealings with Maria Luiz.

Chapter 18

CONTACT

For the first three months, Samantha and Bobby simply followed Elias around, tending to the cattle, horses, and the wheat crop.

They worked twelve-hour days, from sunrise to sunset. But they grew stronger and tanned by the relentless rays of the sun.

Tuesdays and Saturdays were always in-town days. They would gather their food and supplies and speak to Tom at the local market. Tom would often address them as though he was their father.

In his fatherly way, he said to them: "You two take care of yourselves. Tornado season is just around the corner."

Samantha would always pick up any local or national papers. Bobby was spending most of his time with a lovely young thing named Lisa. Bobby adored her—she was just gorgeous. He would spend hours devising ways to attract her, whether it was flowers, candies, music, or his near-beautiful face.

Like an older sister, Sam said, "Get over it. Ask her out on a date—she can only say yes or no."

The next Saturday, Sam told Bobby that she would be going alone into town. She said, "I have to see Dr. Wells."

Bobby was alarmed. He said, "Is there anything wrong? Maybe I should go with you."

"Not necessary," said Samantha. " Just some female stuff. Give me a list of what we need and some cash."

It was taking longer than usual for Sam's return, even with the doctor's appointment. Bobby had butterflies in his stomach. He felt a sigh of relief when he saw Samantha drive under the newly constructed arch over the entrance to the ranch: The Bar SB Ranch.

As she started to unload the truck, Bobby noticed that she had been crying. Bobby was clearly frightened. He stepped right up to Sam and asked, "What's the matter?"

She started to cry again and between sobs said, "Bobby, I'm pregnant!"

Bobby held Samantha in his arms; he hadn't done this since she fell off her bike at ten years old.

Samantha decided it was time to temporarily resurface and contact her father. She texted:

Dear Daddy:

Bobby and I are safe and making ends meet. We live and work on a beautiful little farm. I have learned to ride a horse, herd cattle, and tend to a wheat farm. Quite a difference from university life. But at least I can sleep without those horrible nightmares. There is a big change in my life. I am pregnant. The baby's father is Peter Morris, a buyer and seller of religious antiquities. I love him dearly, he arranged for Bobby and me to disappear. He saved our lives. I feel I will never see him again. I think the baby is a boy and I will name him Peter Stephen James. Bobby already insists we should call him PJ. One day we will need you, but I can't tell you where we are. The orthodox church still believes I am toxic. How is Uncle Jack?

With all of our love,

Bobby and Samantha.

Stephen read the text, tears in his eyes. With regret, he texted Samantha and relayed his encounter with Peter and his surrender of the zip transfer.

When Samantha read her father's text, she was pissed. *Peter has betrayed me,* she thought to herself. But when her sense of calm was restored, she acknowledged that above all, he was trying to protect Bobby and herself.

She really didn't care about the zip transfer; it was merely a backup anyway. Winston Kelly of the Pneumonic Studies Department at USC had inserted a neuromorphic chip in-between her thumb and forefinger. The chip contained all of the information that was stored in the zip transfer.

Late that night, Stephen awoke—something was bothering him about Samantha's text. *Why did she mention Uncle Jack?"* he wondered.

His best friend in college was Jack Wilkinson. Jack had become Bobby and Samantha's make-believe uncle.

"Of course," reasoned Stephen. She is trying to tell me where she is. She was in one of two places: Belize or Oklahoma. No Wilkinson in Belize, but when he googled a Wilkinson in Southwestern Oklahoma, population 8692..."Bingo!" he said out loud.

Chapter 19

BONANZA
AND PJ

There was a knock at the door early one Saturday evening.

"Hello, my name is Charlie Wertz. I am your next-door neighbor. Can I speak to you for a bit?" Charlie asked.

Charlie was short, spectacled, and frail.

"Welcome, my name is Bobby. Come on in," Bobby said.

Samantha was sitting at the fireplace, with her legs raised and resting upon a small stool. Bobby introduced Samantha as his sister and said, "As you can see, she is very, very pregnant."

Dryly, Charlie said, "Congratulations."

Charlie added, "I am a scientist from Orange County, California. Although I have committed no crime, I wish to keep my identity and whereabouts confidential."

"Of course, and we would like you, reciprocally, to honor our confidence," said Samantha.

"Excellent," said Charlie. "Now let me tell you about the point for my visit. A geologist visited my property approximately five months ago. He did some sample testing and felt that our little valley, abutted by the small mountain range, could contain a small oil reservoir.

"The first well I drilled was relatively successful—it is producing forty-five barrels a day. The geologist suggested that I do some slant drilling. I am a man of conscience; the slant drilling encroached on the northeast section of your property. I would propose that we split the slant profits fifty-fifty.

"My only condition is that no one is to know of the owners of this well. I would suggest that we set up a Controlled Foreign Corporation that will be domiciled in the Cayman Islands. No one would be able to ascertain the shareholders, and as long as we report any income from the oil reserves on our personal income tax returns, we should be ok," said Charlie.

"Whatever he just said, I'm in," said Samantha. Bobby agreed wholeheartedly.

"The first slant came in at 100 barrels a day. The second was a monster producing over 400 barrels a day," added Bobby.

Charlie said, "These wells have a moderate decline curve; that is to say, they'll produce but not forever—maybe eight years."

Neither Bobby nor Samantha could have cared less. Each year, Bobby and Samantha drilled new wells on their property and cooperated with Charlie on slants.

Three years after PJ was born, Samantha and Bobby had become multi-millionaires, collecting over $600 thousand per month in oil and gas revenues.

Charlie took care of all of the financial arrangements and disclosures.

"Thank God he is an honest man," said Samantha.

Samantha and Bobby tore down the original home on the property and built two six thousand square foot mansions. One was occupied by Samantha and PJ; the other by Bobby and his lovely new wife, Lisa. Bobby had found the way to her heart— money and lots of it.

They also built a little home for Elias and increased his wage to two thousand dollars per month. Elias thanked them profusely. He thought he had won the lottery.

Samantha would read the late Saturday's *New York Times* edition, leisurely, on Sundays. On this particular Sunday, she saw the headline, "Pope in New York City." She glanced at his picture and noticed a man standing next to him who was identified as his special assistant.

"Goddammit, it's Peter!" Samantha cried out.

Chapter 20

FATHER MARLO

Samantha had located Peter's address in Rome and sent a harmless postcard to him. The front of the postcard showed an expanse of blue sky and the welcome sign to Wilkinson, Oklahoma, population 8692, The Home of the Oklahoma Prairie Chicken. The reverse of the postcard read:

> *Dear Father Morris:*
>
> *I saw your picture in the New York Times. As the Pope's aide, I hope you had a wonderful time in New York City. I have to tell you that you are the mirror image of my four-year-old son.*
>
> *My continuing love—Choggy's Red*

She knew it was dangerous to communicate with Peter but eventually resolved that if you don't make an error or two in your lifetime, you are not making relevant decisions.

Peter received the postcard and was euphoric. Despite the

euphoria, he was concerned about the well-being of Samantha and his son. He immediately destroyed the postcard but imprinted the locale, Wilkinson, Oklahoma, into his memory.

Pope John used his intercom to summon Father Marlo. "Father Marlo, could you please come into my office," said Pope John.

"Of course, Your Holiness," said Father Marlo.

In a moment of déjà vu, Pope John spoke to Farther Marlo. "Father Marlo, this conversation is extremely sensitive and most confidential," said Pope John. The Pope had a stern look on his face.

The Pope recounted the details of the saga of Samantha James, the Qumran Cave discovery, Professor el-Zebn, and Peter Morris's pursuit of the zip transfer.

"Certain information has come to my attention that is contradicting Father Morris's reports. Painfully, I am asking you and our electronic surveillance team to carefully search Father Morris's apartment. I want to see if he still holds the zip transfer. Oh Lord, please let me be in the wrong," said the Pope. He made the sign of the cross and raised his eyes to the heavens in a virtuous, reverent gesture.

It was a small apartment and Father Marlo and his team were repeatedly bumping into each other. The search had reached a near microscopic level—medicinal capsules were opened, toothpaste dispensers were searched, even sheets of toilet paper were carefully examined. They found nothing.

Father Marlo turned to the shredded mattress on the bed and for the sixth or seventh time opened the drawer of the bed stand. It contained only the Holy Bible. In anger as he slammed the drawer shut, he heard the wisp of a clanking sound.

He removed the Holy Bible and found a false bottom in the drawer. He pried open the bottom and found a .38 revolver. Father Marlo carefully opened the chamber and found five bullets and an electronic device.

Moments later, one of the surveillance team members saw Peter approaching the apartment building. He barked, "Let's get out of here. Father Peter is on his way up."

Father Marlo and his team used the back stairs to escape detection.

Peter opened the door to chaos. He knew what they were looking for. Did they find it? He saw his .38 on the bed along with five bullets.

He threw the .38, the bullets, and anything else of value into a small suitcase marked with the insignia of Pope John. He hoped that the insignia would discourage Security from reviewing its contents. He felt that he might need his revolver.

Within an hour, Father Marlo entered the Pope's office, zip transfer in hand.

"You have done an excellent job, Father Marlo," said Pope John. "But I must admit this discovery saddens me. 1 have lost my rock. My rock has now become an adversary of the Mother Church. And what a penance he will pay."

The Pope turned to Father Marlo and said, "We must thank the Lord for the vast network of informants that tend to our needs. One such informant, working in the United States Department of the Treasury, matched the social security number on income tax filings of one Samantha James, an archaeologist in Los Angeles, with an oil and gas developer living in some wretched place called Wilkinson, Oklahoma. Father Morris assured me he had dealt with Ms. James while in Belize. Apparently, Father Morris was in error. I'm sure you will find Father Morris and his whore in Wilkinson.

"There are too many loose ends in the Qumran Cave matter. I expect you to deal with these loose ends, Father Marlo. Do you understand me?" asked Pope John.

Father Marlo replied, "Of course, Your Holiness."

Pope John sensed reticence in Father Marlo's voice.

As Marlo walked to the door, Pope John said firmly, "Don't disappoint Mother Church. If you have any problems whatsoever, contact Father Timothy."

"There will be no problems, Your Holiness," said Father Marlo.

Father Marlo had never been in the Pope's private jet. Nor had he ever carried a revolver in his vest with an intent to commit murder. He perspired profusely, but remembered the Pope's parting words, "Don't disappoint Mother Church."

He drifted off to sleep on the long journey over the ocean once he had convinced himself that he was on a mission from God.

Chapter 21

CONFLICT IN OKLAHOMA

It was a lazy Friday afternoon and Samantha had just completed her homeschooling of PJ. At five years of age, he was surprisingly tall. He was also very bright—he was already reading at the sixth-grade level.

Bobby was outside polishing his new Porsche Turbo Carrera, when a car drove onto the circular driveway.

A large man opened the car door. Bobby immediately recognized him—it was Peter.

Bobby said, "Peter, what are you doing here?"

Peter was amazed by the size and elegance of the compound. "But these are merely things—beautiful, but only things," Peter thought aloud.

Peter asked, "Where is Samantha? We need to talk."

Sensing that Peter was in a hurry, Bobby ushered him to the front door and quickly opened it.

Peter saw that Samantha's appearance had not changed.

She was even more beautiful than he remembered.

Instead of striking Peter for all of the lost moments, Samantha found herself rushing into his arms. They kissed longingly but in a split second Samantha dragged him to meet his son, PJ.

Samantha introduced PJ to his father and PJ responded, "I am glad to meet you, sir. My mother has told me a great deal about you."

Peter's eyes filled with tears as he bent down to hug PJ; the hug seemed to last an eternity. As Samantha began to cry, Bobby teared up.

Samantha, tears still in her eyes, whispered, "Peter, why are you here?"

Peter stared directly at both Bobby and Samantha and said:

"We must leave immediately. They have found the zip transfer and although they can destroy the evidence, the trail of assassinations and their inability to determine exactly what you know leaves them no choice. Our total and complete escape could eventually lead to the demise of the Roman Catholic Church as we know it today.

"Pack light, quickly, and call an Uber driver. Tell him that we will have six passengers and need to be taken to the Tulsa airport," added Peter.

Before anyone could move, Father Marlo exploded through

the front door. Revolver in hand, he roared, "Everyone, hands on your head and no quick movements."

Even PJ followed Father Marlo's instructions.

Father Marlo collected himself and said in a bleak tone, "I will try to make this as quick as possible."

Samantha carefully placed PJ behind her back.

Father Marlo continued, "I am sorry that it had to end this way—especially for you, Father Morris, and the child. Father Morris, you were Pope John's rock. As you know, Father Morris, at the head of every household is a man; at the head of man is Christ; at the head of every woman is a man; at the head of Christ is God. There is no room in our world for a woman God."

"Wait!" said Peter. "You may take my life, for as the Pope's rock, I will most certainly find a place in hell. But Samantha, her son, and brother are innocents. They know nothing of the contents of the zip transfer. If you kill them, you will accompany me on a grueling path to a place for the punishment of the wicked," added Peter.

"I apologize, Father Morris, but the Pope was quite explicit—there are too many loose ends in this matter. I must do my duty," said Father Marlo.

As he raised his revolver to Samantha's head, he muttered, "God forgive me."

Peter quickly pushed Samantha aside and accepted the

bullet in her stead. Peter never had a chance to remove the revolver from his pocket. Samantha screamed as she saw Peter fall to the floor.

As Father Marlo raised his revolver again, Samantha closed her eyes, anticipating a bullet that was to end her life. There was a shot, but she felt no pain.

Father Marlo's head had been blown off from behind. With smoking gun in hand, her father, Stephen James, stood at the front door. He had promised he would never kill again, but he had no choice.

Samantha was cradling both PJ and Peter. She tried to cover PJ's eyes so that he couldn't see the blood cascading from his father's wound.

Stephen James reverted to his cop-like persona and instantly began to issue instructions.

"Samantha," he said, "I'll deal with this scumbag's body and only because of my love for you and my grandson, I'll take care of Peter. That is, if he survives. Never cared much for the son-of-a-bitch. If the Catholic Church hierarchy is involved in this Qumran matter—and I think they are—Peter may be wanted by clerical and pedestrian cops around the world for the rest of his life. If he lives, we will need to become invisible.

"You must expose this Qumran Cave manuscript as quickly as possible and, for your own protection, hire 24-7 security for all of you. It looks like you can afford it."

As Bobby and Stephen lifted Peter from the floor, he opened his eyes to see Samantha. Peter whispered, 'I love you. You must find Maria Luiz. She is somewhere in Brazil."

Chapter 22

EXPOSURE AND PJ'S DEPARTURE

S amantha had the neuromorphic chip removed from her hand and the plates were once again developed by a small army of cryptographers and translators.

She chose her friend, Julie Myers, the editor of the *Los Angeles Times,* to tell her controversial and twisted story.

The headline read:

IS GOD A WOMAN?

POPE INDICTED ON ACCESSORY TO MURDER CHARGES
POPE'S AIDE MISSING

Pope John labeled Samantha as wicked and delusional. Eventually, Samantha's saga became indisputable as the plethora of facts were divulged. Although Pope John could not be extradited, political pressures within the Catholic Church led to his resignation as well as the resignation of substantially all of the religious aristocracy in Vatican City.

Many Catholics continued to believe that His Holiness, Pope John, was the true moral and righteous leader of the Catholic Church. But with the discovery of the Qumran Cave 12 plates, the affairs of the world were spinning out of control and changing at an exponential rate.

All religions of the world were impacted, but the Catholic Church suffered the most violent upheaval.

One year after the Qumran Cave 12 revelations, females were allowed to be ordained Catholic priests, deacons, and bishops. More importantly, after two years of bitter controversy Pope Ana was elected by the Papal Conclave to become the 269th Pope and its first female to hold such an office.

Those Catholics that believed in the admissions of the Qumran Cave 12 manuscripts, for no apparent reason, sighed in relief and were enveloped by a sense of calm once Ana was named Pope.

No longer were women in the Catholic Church considered incapable of fulfilling their religious roles without the aid of a man.

Visibility does breed justice.

In the midst of controversy surrounding the clerical world, Samantha had her own personal issues to deal with. One such issue was temporarily resolved when she received a text from her father:

> **Samantha,**
>
> *PJ is recovering but it will be a long process. Don't call my cell unless it's an absolute emergency. Less communication, the better. Tell Bobby I love him.*
>
> *Love, Daddy.*

A most difficult decision involved the schooling of PJ. Bobby was relentless in his recommendation that PJ needed to be schooled amongst his peers.

Samantha knew instinctively that Bobby was right and located a boarding school in Switzerland that tended to children of political figures and the wealthy. Samantha finally capitulated when she realized that the students could be accompanied by personal security guards.

As she put PJ on the plane, she sobbed uncontrollably. She went home and locked herself inside and continued to cry and cry and cry. *Now, both of them are gone,* she thought.

Two weeks after PJ's departure, Samantha heard a ghastly banging on the door. It was Bobby.

Bobby, uncharacteristically, raised his voice and said, "You look like hell and you must have lost thirty pounds. Dad didn't raise you to be a sniveling little bastard. Get your goddamned act together! Nothing will work unless you do."

Then Bobby held her tightly, kissed her on the cheek, and walked away. She had known it all along—action is a remedy for sorrow.

Chapter 23

THE LORD GOD

Peter had pleaded with Samantha to locate a Maria Luiz apparently located somewhere in Brazil. Maria Luiz claimed to have been visited by a woman Lord God. It took a small fortune to locate Maria in the southern jungles of Brazil, but Samantha found her. Samantha then wrote a letter to Maria, asking if she could visit with her. Weeks later, Maria responded in broken English:

> *Ms. James,*
>
> *I would very much like to meet you. You are very famous and we have much in common. When you come, you stay in my house. It is very small and there is much children, but I have an extra bed.*
>
> *Much cordial,*
> *Maria Luiz.*

When they met, they became immediate friends: Maria, speaking in her broken English and Samantha responding in poquito Español. They were a pair and seemed to communicate as if they had always known each other. Samantha experienced a sense of calm when she was with Maria.

Samantha, of course, wanted to learn of the visitation by the female Lord God. Maria reluctantly recounted the terrifying words of Father Morris. Samantha had never seen this side of Peter and was careful not to tell Maria of their relationship.

Eventually, Maria secretly told Samantha she would often see her Lord God walking amongst the fields. Despite her degree in theological studies and her discovery of the Qumran Cave 12 manuscript, Samantha was still skeptical.

At twilight each day, Maria and Samantha would head toward the fields. They would talk mostly about silly girl stuff. They had bonded.

After nearly a month of trudging to the fields, Samantha spotted a middle-aged woman dressed in jeans, a blossomy top, and tennis shoes. Samantha thought she looked like a typical woman who had just picked up her children from soccer practice. She had a beautiful smile and a sensuous glow about her face.

Maria called to Samantha, "There She is!"

The closer She came, the greater the sense of calm that enveloped Samantha

Samantha said, "You can't be…"

The Lord God responded, "Just about the only one you'll ever get. What did you expect—beauty incarnate?"

The Lord God turned to Maria and said in Spanish, "I had to add a little fertilizer to the fruit trees—they were looking a little tired."

She looked to Samantha and said, "Thank you for bringing my existence to the forefront. I tried to help you as much as I could, but I am generally a hands-off type. The only help I could really offer was to ensure that you lived to reveal your saga. That is why I brought you back to life after you fell to your death in the Qumran Cave 12."

"But how can you appear and act so commonplace?" asked Samantha.

She replied, "Because I am you and you are me." She continued, "Throughout the universe, the people of Earth have proven to be an intelligent lot, but they are also the most perverse and stubborn. I try to bring you peace and tranquility but all you want to do is kill each other. What will I ever do with you?"

"What can we do to help?" asked Samantha.

"It's really simple," she said. "Just try to love each other—even the damned lady next door who owns the dog that barks at night. Lighten up! There is more to life than always attempting to increase its speed."

"Not everyone sings the ballads of peace composed by John Lennon; all-encompassing love is a tough sell," Samantha said.

The Lord God responded, "You'll eventually figure out a way to come to some meaningful form of resolution. And by the way, I didn't like John Lennon—he was an atheist. Stick with Paul—he's easier to digest."

As the Lord God turned to walk away, she said to Samantha and Maria, "Maybe one day we can all meet again to speak of things to come."

She disappeared into the rays of the setting sun.

From that day forward, Samantha stopped listening to John Lennon's music.

Chapter 24

S andra Wells had the look of a devout Mormon: blond hair, blue eyes, and a complexion that never fancied the taste of alcohol, tobacco, or caffeine. She believed that the future came one day at a time and that the Church of Jesus Christ of Latter Day Saints was the true restoration of the original church founded by Jesus Christ. Under a doctrine of continuing education, she also believed that its president was a modern-day prophet, seer, and revelator of the word of Jesus Christ.

Although Sandra could not be ordained into the Mormon priesthood, she held leadership roles, at a very young age, in a number of the Church's auxiliary organizations. She was proud of the fact that the LDS Church stressed worldwide humanitarian service and violently discounted claims of Mormon haters who believed that the church indulged in historical revisionism, homophobia, racism, and sexist policies.

She paid little attention when the church took a prominent role in opposing the Equal Rights Amendment and the perceived heresy of the Qumran Cave 12 Manuscript.

The then-President of the Church of Jesus Christ of Latter Day Saints would consider Sandra the quintessential Mormon woman.

At age twenty, and although it was not required, Sandra served a two-year full-time proselytizing mission, attempting to convert the Pueblo tribe of Native Americans to Mormonism. It was a hot, crusty environment in New Mexico but she appeared to be making inroads. The native Indians would listen intently and often shake their heads in assent when she spoke of Mormon ideas, including the most important event, purportedly, in human history—Joseph Smith's first vision at an early age by two heavenly personages, God the Father and his son, Jesus Christ.

At night around the campfire, the tribal elders would tell of their early religion prior to the coming of the Franciscan Friars. The elders spoke of a simple set of beliefs, orchestrated by two sisters—one went to the east and became the Mother of the White People; the other became the Mother of the Indians.

The Sisters encouraged people to treat each other with kindness and respect within a web of complete equality amongst men and women, white men, Indians, and other people of color.

The Sisters were also practical, for they taught the Pueblos to preserve their lands so that they might control nature for their own purposes. In all of the Sisters' teachings, there were no words for money or wealth, power or influence.

After consuming the convictions of the Pueblo elders over the course of two years, there was an implosion of the neurons and synapses in Sandra's brain. It was all so simple! She became less than the quintessential Mormon woman.

Sandra had read of Samantha James and called Samantha to, hopefully, arrange a meeting in Wilkinson, Oklahoma. Although Samantha was initially reticent, she was overcome by Sandra's engaging enthusiasm.

Samantha finally said to the near-Mormon, "Sure, come on down to the Bar SB Ranch. We're just outside of Tulsa."

Samantha spent nearly a week with Sandra discussing her archaeological background, the Qumran Cave adventure, professor Elezar el-Zebn, and her escape from the clutches of the Catholic Church. She introduced Sandra to Maria, who along with her family had moved to the Bar SB Ranch, and carefully spoke of their encounter with the woman Lord God; Sandra felt like a young child on Christmas Eve.

Sandra began to sense a stunning similarity between the teachings of the Pueblo Sisters and the woman Lord God. As her Mormonism continued to dissolve, Sandra was eager to tell of her newfound sense of conviction.

Just as Sandra was about to leave the Bar SB Ranch, Samantha, in a mother–daughter fashion, said to Sandra, "Sweetheart, I want you to be very careful with your exuberance. Affirming a woman Lord God can be perilous—especially with the people in Salt Lake City. Only a small minority of your people believe in the Qumran Cave 12 Manuscript." Samantha quickly added, "If you ever run into trouble, call my father—he was a former badassed cop. Here is his cell number."

Sandra responded, "Don't worry about me. I mean no one harm. Besides, my husband is an FBI agent."

Samantha couldn't tell if she had blessed or cursed the young Sandra.

***

Jack Wells was a stand-up FBI agent. He was a perfect fit for the Bureau—intelligent, capable of handling firearms, and a clean-cut Mormon. No one really knew, however, that he was actually a Jack-Mormon—one that skirted most of the strict directives of the LDS church. Jack was only dedicated to his lovely wife, Sandra, and would honor her every wish.

When Sandra returned to Salt Lake City, she began to sponsor teas in which she spoke of her benign religious philosophies. She had no intent or desire to proselytize—she merely spoke of a simple religion that stressed the consideration we should afford each other. At the first tea she hosted, it produced two guests—a young, female adolescent and her husband. By word-of-mouth, the teas eventually turned into Sunday meetings in a rented hall. Surprisingly, men began to attend.

She didn't ask for a tithe nor was a collection plate passed among the members. Nevertheless, the new members began to make voluntary contributions, and sizeable ones at that.

Late one night after a Sunday meeting, there was a crash that blasted through Jack and Sandra's bedroom window. Their bedroom was suddenly afire and Sandra's legs were instantly incinerated. Jack, blanket in hand, attempted to extinguish the fire from Sandra's legs and ran through the front door. As he sat her on the front yard grass, he watched his home burn to the ground.

Jack screamed, "I am going to kill these bastards. Like Abraham Lincoln, I may walk slowly, but I never walk backward."

While Sandra was in the hospital, Jack began to read the unopened mountain of mail addressed to Sandra. Most of it was hideous hate mail condemning her belief in a woman Lord God. Several letters were signed by Senegoid. They were the most monstrous—he spoke of early Apache tortures where she would be repeatedly raped and just near death, a lance would be thrust into her sweet spot until it finally exited her skull.

The Salt Lake City branch of the FBI was useless in its attempts to discover the identity of the suspect—or suspects—that had firebombed the Wells's home. But Jack was relentless. He wouldn't let it go. Over and over again, the location of Senegoid rumbled through his head. He used every sophisticated form of FBI-created investigative technique. But nothing! He didn't want this case to end up in the stack of dead files.

He had the Senegoid file on his desk when his partner, Brian Lamley, sat down across from him.

"Anything?" asked Brian.

"Not a goddamned—excuse me—damned thing," said Jack.

Looking at the file upside down, Brian said, "Well maybe you're looking for the wrong man. Senegoid spelled backwards is Diogenes. I think Diogenes is a Greek historical figure that was in a perpetual search for an honest man."

"Brian, I think you are a genius," said Jack.

Instantly, Jack went online to link Diogenes to a Salt Lake City source. There was one distinctive match: a Diogenes, Inc. Diogenes, Inc. was a financial services firm headed by a Mahlon Kearns.

He had a license plate that read:

DIOGENES 1

Kearns was a distinguished deacon in the Mormon Church who apparently had a white-hot temper.

With a search warrant, Jack had secured Kearns's bank

records, along with several handwritten pieces of correspondence directed to his friend, Peter Calhoun, the president of Zion Bank.

He took the correspondence, along with Sandra's letters to Brian. Brian doubled as a handwriting specialist in the Salt Lake Bureau. Brian confronted Jack an hour later and said, "They're a perfect match."

Jack didn't want to take any chances. The headline read:

Financial Executive Found Hung in an Apparent Suicide

Brian Lamley walked past Jack's desk the next morning and said, "I'm sure you read of Kearns's suicide. I know you will have a rock-solid alibi, but I think we should keep the Diogenes matter amongst ourselves."

"Of course," said Jack. But Jack really didn't care if he was found out—he just wanted the bastard dead and buried.

There were no more letters from Senegoid.

As Sandra healed, she began to speak at Sunday meetings once again. Her beautiful legs were always covered by blue jeans.

Sandra's dogged determination resulted in success, for three years later she became the leader of the New Church of Lord God which was represented by over 500,000 members in 47 churches throughout the United States. Her word had taken hold.

During services, the music of Paul McCartney played in the background.

The Church of the Latter-Day Saints, much like the Catholic Church, was facing a draconian irritant.

Chapter 25

A BONDING

They decided to meet in Prague, the capital and largest city in the Czech Republic. The apartment building was a dark and dingy high-rise, built in the 1990s. The building was across from the Astronomical Clock in Old Town.

The meeting was held in Room 765. The room was still covered in mold from the widespread floods of 2002. The room had a single, small table and two dilapidated chairs in the center. The only light was provided by a single bulb dropped from a four-foot cord from the ceiling. Rats scurried between the walls in an endless search for morsels of food.

The smell in the room was hideous. It was a less than ambitious location for such an historic meeting.

Outside the rooms were four members of the exclusive Pontifical Swiss Guard.

John was stout and bald. Russell was slim with a full head of hair and appeared as though he had spent a great deal of time in the sun.

John was the first to speak. "I would never have conceived of such a meeting—our viewpoints are, at best, diverse. But these are difficult times and require extraordinary measures. It may be our last chance to eradicate the acts of transgression against divine law.

"Our combined financial resources were once equivalent to a super-sized Amazon. Now our members, missionaries and coffers continue to dwindle. Shortly, I fear we will become only a footnote to recorded narratives," explained John.

Russell strained to see John's face in the dim light and powerfully responded, "I suggest that we direct our energies on answers, not excuses for our potential demise. God is our driving rod, but let's not fool ourselves. We are here to address our need for elements essential to the dissemination of the Word of God—specifically, wealth, power and influence."

John was taken aback by Russell's direct, but almost abusive, response.

Nevertheless, as embarrassed as John was, he responded. "I will take care of the three targets by myself. They will never be found in the Vatican Necropolis that lies under the Vatican City. It's understandable how fragile the archeological excavations have become in recent years—especially in the area surrounding the grave of Peter the Apostle. A cave-in might occur at any moment. Of course, it is possible that I could be immersed by such a landslide along with the three targets—Samantha, Maria and Sandra. My sainthood is clearly on hold, but we must rid ourselves of the targets that have initiated an offense against the Church by despising His person."

"I'm sure our God will be proud of your sacrifice, John, and I will applaud your actions in my prayers. I will, however, not sacrifice my life in this venture, for God has spoken to me and renounced any such action. Nevertheless, I will be very direct in my part. I'll destroy all 47 sites of the false New Lord of God Church. There will be no evidence of my complicity in these actions. There are several Mormons in the Federal Bureau of Investigation who will do my bidding. And, by the way, have the four guards outside killed. I want no one to be acquainted with this meeting," Russell said.

The former Pope John and the President of the Church of Jesus Christ of Latter Day Saints, Russell Newton, had bonded the Catholic and Mormon ministries.

Chapter 26

CHARLIE AND THE RANCH

The fields of wheat had years ago been replaced by operating oil wells, but the ranch still had a small apple grove. Samantha and Maria often walked through the grove picking the ripest apples. This was the best of times for Maria. Maria always had an apple corer in her hand. She made apple pies, apple cakes, apple dumplings, and applesauce. Bobby's children, as well as her own, were her favorite customers.

During the course of their walks in the apple grove, Samantha and Maria never came upon the woman Lord God. Maria prayed each night that she would see Her at least one more time in her life.

Maria's husband, Rodriguez, assisted Bobby with the ranch affairs. He was especially adept in dealing with the oil rig machinery, for he grew up in the business. His father was a roughneck on wells in Brazil. Rodriguez was also very familiar with secondary recovery techniques. He eventually convinced Bobby to inject steam in the oldest wells to enhance their production despite the fact that they were reaching the ebb of the decline curve.

The production on these wells did, in fact, increase dramatically and, as a reward, Bobby purchased a silver 1500 Dodge Ram for Rodriguez. The truck was tricked out with every convenience known to man. Rodriguez lovingly washed the truck every day except on Sunday, the Lord's Day. When he had an opportunity to drive his truck, he would blast Latin music from his souped-up sound system. Bobby reached the point when he became quite the fan of this musical genre.

Their next-door neighbor, Charlie, would visit with Samantha and Bobby at the end of each month to discuss production, per barrel prices, and other financial affairs. Charlie's news was, more often than not, always a source of bliss. More production, more wells, and more money. This month he was a week early, and he had a stern look on his face.

He looked to Samantha and Bobby and said, "I'm in a bit of trouble and will have to leave very shortly. I have come to ask if you would like to purchase my ranch and the oil and gas properties. I only have 200 acres, plus or minus a few, but there are over 60 wells, including the slants, and I am netting approximately $5 million per year, after taxes. There is also the possibility that an additional 30 wells could be drilled on the property. Oil and gas properties usually sell for 3 to 5 times their annual net, but as I said, I'm in a hurry. If you can arrange for a purchase within a week or so, I would be willing to sell you the property for $5 million."

"Absolutely not," stated Samantha with heavy emphasis. "I won't pay you anything less than $7.5 million. Just give me wiring instructions and I'll have the transfer made this afternoon."

"Both of you are too kind," said Charlie as he handed his Swiss bank account number to Samantha.

"What kind of trouble are you in?" asked Bobby. "Maybe we can help."

"I don't think anyone can help me," Charlie replied. "My contacts tell me that the Federal Agents are closing in."

"Federal Agents!" exclaimed Bobby. "That sounds like serious business."

"Yes, it's serious business." responded Charlie. "I have harmed no one nor stolen anything. My trouble is centered about a critical piece of knowledge I hold," added Charlie.

Samantha thought to herself, *Sounds familiar.*

Charlie was beginning to break down and said, "Oh, what the hell. You'll find out about it eventually. I am a Harvard-educated scientist with an advanced degree in cybernetics.

In connection with the Associate Director of Neuromorphic Studies at USC, Dr. Winston Kelly, we developed an advanced neurological chip that one day could lead to singularity."

Samantha inadvertently gasped as she remembered her relationship with Winston and the chip that he had placed in between her thumb and forefinger.

"Pardon my ignorance," said Bobby, "but what the hell is singularity?"

Charlie continued. "I know it sounds like geeky science fiction stuff, but this chip could actually initiate artificial intelligence. Inserting this chip into a supercomputer could allow this computer the capability to create a better version of itself— over and over and over again. Such a duplication process could conceivably result in singularity—a concept where machines become exponentially smarter than humans. These computers, if left unmonitored, could spin out of control and dramatically alter human civilization.

"Winston felt that singularity would initially create a worldwide economic collapse by eliminating all practical jobs and create rampant unemployment which would cause consumer demand to implode.

"Following an economic collapse, singularity could simply treat the human race as an unwanted irritant and ultimately lead to its demise. Our destiny would then be in the hands of a God, if there is one.

"The agents must be close. Winston has gone into hiding, but he heard from his sources at USC that they ransacked his lab yesterday. Eventually the agents will establish a link between Winston and me. I don't want to waste any time," Charlie added with a heightened sense of urgency. Charlie began to sob and said, "I don't care what you think, but I am gay, and Winston and I are lovers. I miss him desperately."

Samantha rushed to hug Charlie and whispered to him, "I know Winston. He was a great help to me."

Taken aback, Charlie stumbled and said, "How could you? When did you know him?"

Samantha whispered again, "That's a story for another day. We have got to get you out of here. Bobby will drive you to the airport and explain where you should end up."

Samantha went to the safe and removed $100,000. She told Charlie, "Take this—it should help you get settled."

Charlie, with tears in his eyes, kissed both Samantha and Bobby. Samantha and Charlie never had a chance to discuss that "another-day story." Charlie committed suicide.

Chapter 27

CATE AND SPRING BREAK

S amantha sent PJ to Cate in Switzerland, one of the oldest American boarding schools in Europe. Its student body was comprised of 900 students and represented by 50 nationalities.

The prestigious school was nestled amongst a hillside in sunny Switzerland with spectacular views of snow-capped mountains and palm trees. Cate encouraged cross-border experiences intended to teach students about the rich and colorful cultural heritage of Europe.

Samantha was sold on Cate when she discovered that PJ could be accompanied by a personal security guard. With all of its trappings, Cate had a price to match: $86,800 per year. There were also additional fees to feed and house the security guard, if one was required.

Although extremely intelligent, PJ had just a B-average

because he applied himself only when he was truly interested in a subject. He had only two great loves. One was debating. PJ became the leader of the Debate Team and, even though he was not a true believer, he had an amazing ability to debate the principles of theology. His second love, like most young men, was the interscholastic athletic programs. PJ would often send Samantha copies of the school newspaper where his skiing exploits were memorialized. There was talk that one day he might be an Olympic alpine skier. He was also captain of the Lacrosse Team and a fiery competitor. Sometimes too fiery.

PJ had thick blond hair that was cropped like his father. Although he was only thirteen, he was five feet, eleven inches tall and a lean 150 pounds. His shoes were a size 14, indicating that he would eventually be well over six feet tall. He was a hit with girls, but only dated girls that were sixteen or seventeen. They were dramatically more developed. He was his father's twin.

Although PJ for the most part enjoyed Cate, he often felt imprisoned by the spartan living quarters and the restrictions of a formal dress code.

Duke, PJ's private security guard, was a big old Marine who fought with Bobby in Pakistan. He had a face that looked like he could eat you, but he had the heart of a loving puppy.

Duke had three special loves: PJ, the Semper Fi ring on his

finger, and Corona Extra that he would drink in excess when sitting with Bobby. Bobby and Duke would sit up all night glorifying their war memories. After one of these sessions, Bobby would be in bed for at least a day or two. Duke would wake up early and open another Corona; amazingly, he was never hungover.

Duke dealt with mostly close-quarter protection of PJ from the first class to lights out. Although he didn't wear body armor, he carried an expandable baton and a Beretta .92. He was also an expert in unarmed combat and had a bunch of first aid training. He was a formidable force to deal with.

Most of the Cate students, on occasion, were capable of eluding their security guards—it was more of a game to them. But Duke could not be outwitted, no matter how well-planned or conceived by PJ. Even after the most circuitous of routes, Duke was always there, just waiting for him. PJ was baffled.

PJ was chronically itching the spot between his forefinger and thumb. The school physician at Cate simply prescribed an antibiotic ointment that PJ was to administer three times a day. But it never worked. PJ did not realize that Winston, as a favor to his mother, had chipped him right after his birth. Duke had a receiver tuned to the frequency of his neuromorphic chip. Samantha and Bobby had the same receiver. Samantha had her receiver at hand, 24-7.

Spring break was rapidly approaching and PJ could hardly wait to be home where he could ride horses, drive some cattle, and just do some plain old Oklahoma shit-kicking.

Samantha and Maria had cleaned PJ's room three times, set out his favorite jeans, boots, and hat. The final class at Cate was on early Tuesday.

Samantha instructed Richard, the pilot of their Cessna Citation X, to pick up Duke and PJ as soon as they were able to assemble their gear. Samantha estimated that they should be home, as usual, at approximately 9:00 p.m.

Samantha's cell rang—it was Richard. "Sam, we're having some pretty nasty weather on this side. I don't think we'll be able to take off until tomorrow morning. I'll keep you apprised."

It was Wednesday night and still no PJ, Duke, or Richard. She tried all of their cells and there was no response. Panic was setting in. Samantha had spoken to her father and Peter only sporadically in recent years, but she felt this required a 911 response, even though Peter would have to come to the surface.

"Daddy, this is Sam. Something's terribly wrong," she said. "PJ, Richard, and Duke are MIA. I can't raise them by phone and PJ's chip is not responding to my receiver." Samantha was now sobbing uncontrollably.

Stephen took control of the conversation: "It will take Peter and me six hours or so to be at the ranch. Remember Sam, the best way to get out of a bad situation is to go through it. Believe me, we will get through it together," Stephen reassured her.

Even her father's counsel, though, could not bring Sam down. As Samantha hung up, she pleaded, "Daddy, please hurry!"

Just then, Samantha heard a truck enter the driveway. "Thank God," she said excitedly. "He's finally home!"

Unfortunately, it wasn't PJ and Duke—it was a FedEx driver. The driver handed Samantha a small box. She opened the package to find a gold box with Pope John's insignia.

As she opened the box, she screamed in terror and fainted. Inside the box was Duke's finger and his Semper Fi ring, attached with a note that read:

Ms. James: Be at the Vatican City Gardens along with Mrs. Luiz next Tuesday at 9:00 a.m. If you don't comply or you contact the authorities, you will never see your son again.

Chapter 28

KIDNAPPED

Bobby and Samantha had purchased a Cessna Citation X. They didn't really need a private jet. It was purchased principally to transport PJ back and forth from Cate. Although Duke was a licensed pilot, the flying of the Cessna was left to Richard Simmons.

Richard was a retired Air Force pilot who had fought in Afghanistan, Iraq, and, most recently, in the Pakistan affair. He was a typical pilot, clean-shaven and strikingly handsome with a tint of grey in his hair. Every now and then Samantha would even take a second look.

Richard was shot down in Afghanistan and was housed in a rebel's prison camp for almost six months. He walked with a limp—the Afghan rebels were notorious for their methods of torture. Richard never spoke to anyone about his six-month imprisonment.

Richard landed in Rome late on Monday in anticipation of a Tuesday flight home once PJ's classes ended at Cate.

On Monday night, a violent storm rolled off the Atlantic into the western coast of Europe. If he was alone, he would have taken the chance and flown home late Tuesday afternoon. But there was PJ and Duke to consider. Richard called Samantha, explained the weather conditions, and anticipated that they would not be able to take off until sometime Wednesday afternoon. He could sense the alarm in her voice.

Richard had used the Vicenza cleaning crew a number of times in the past and, without reservation, handed them the entry keys to the Cessna. Richard found a hotel next to the airport, had a drink, some dinner, and turned in early.

The weather had cleared. PJ and Duke took a limousine to the boarding steps of the Cessna. Duke did not conduct his usual pre-takeoff inspection of the plane. Everyone was in a hurry to get back to Wilkinson.

Thirty minutes after takeoff, Duke peered out the window of the plane and noticed that they were heading in a northerly direction rather than the direct route west.

Irritated, Duke ripped off his seat belt and stormed into the pilot's compartment.

"Goddammit, Richard, where are you?"

Duke could see the garrote around Richard's neck—his eyes were bulging, and his face was deadly purple.

"Come in, Duke," said the pilot. "I am your new pilot, Father Timothy. We will be making a short stop in Rome."

Duke immediately reached for his Beretta .92.

Unphased by the Beretta, Father Timothy said, "Duke, I want you to listen to me carefully. You have three alternatives: Shoot me and my hand will be released from the pressure point on the two grenades at my waist and we will all die. Don't surrender your weapon and I'll take the plane into the ground at 600 miles per hour and we all die; or hand me your gun and we all live. It's your choice."

Duke yelled, "You wouldn't be crazy enough to commit suicide."

Father Timothy replied, "I am by no means crazy, but I am bound to fulfill my duty to the Lord God."

The altimeter read 15,000 feet. Timothy tuned the nose of the plane into a dive—13,000…10,000…6,000…5,000…3,000…2,000…feet until impact.

Duke screamed, "Pull up, pull up, you crazy bastard!" Duke dropped his gun.

Timothy leveled off and gently lifted the Cessna back up to the 15,000-foot level again.

"Now sit down, Duke," said Timothy. "We will be landing in twenty minutes,"

PJ had been tumbled a bit during the rapid descent of the Cessna, but he, like his father, was unflappable in stressful situations.

Duke said to PJ, "Just do what they ask. Whoever they may be, they are deadly serious. The chronic itching between your thumb and forefinger is where a neuro-morphic chip was inserted shortly after your birth by Winston Kelly. He chipped you as a favor to your mother. Eventually your mother and Bobby will be able to track your whereabouts with their chip receivers. These people will have little need for me and will probably kill me once we land."

"What do they want, Duke?" inquired PJ. "If it's money, I'm sure my mother can meet their demands," said PJ.

"I don't think it's money, PJ," said Peter. "But as I said before, just do whatever they ask of you. Hide this small jackknife in your shoe—it's razor-sharp and deadly. Use it only when you have no other alternative. Do you understand me?" cautioned Duke.

"Yes sir," said PJ.

As they exited the plane, a black hood was placed over PJ's head. There were quiet voices and then a muffled shot. PJ heard Duke moan and he began to tear up. He knew this was not the time to reach for his knife—at least not yet.

Chapter 29

CAPTIVE

The clank of the bars indicated that he was in a cell. The cold, musty smell of ancient earth also told him he was underground. Hands against the bars and wall, PJ measured his new home to be eight feet by twelve feet. Not so bad, he thought to himself. *Just about the size of my room at Cate*, he mused.

The only piece of furniture in the cell was a small bed accompanied by an even smaller blanket. He had his travel-home dress on—shorts and a tee shirt. He wished that a small heater was available. Jokingly, he thought, *I wonder if there is room service here?*

Three times a day they would give him a cold pasta dish. It was decent but not from the Ritz. The server said nothing but smelled old. They also provided him with a jug of water and a pot to pee in.

The first two days he fitfully slept on and off. He knew he was sleeping most of the day and night that he could not see.

PJ was convinced they were drugging either his food or the

water. He limited his intake of the water—just enough to stay alive. With the reduced water consumption, he didn't sleep as much and actually became coherent.

Becoming coherent was not exactly a trip to Paris, for he was forced to think in the dark. He thought about an impending death, Duke's demise, and his depressing surroundings. But when he decided to concentrate on lighthearted thoughts, he would think of the Bar SB Ranch in Wilkinson and mostly of his mother.

Three days after the kidnapping, someone removed PJ's hood. The light of a candle held by an old man seared his open eyes. Once he adjusted to the candlelight, he could see the wrinkled face of an old man who was dressed in a vestment. *More likely than not*, thought PJ, *he is a Catholic Priest.*

The old man said, "I know you're frightened but…"

PJ quickly interrupted the old man and said, "Don't flatter yourself. I'm not frightened. As you probably know, one who fears to suffer will always suffer in fear."

"You are arguably as fearless and well-spoken as your father, PJ. You may call me John," said the old man.

"Don't mention my father," insisted PJ. "You didn't know him. He would never have associated with your type of filth. It may be that the collection of your garbage led to his death. Otherwise, why would you have me kidnapped? One day, believe me, I will exact revenge," PJ roared.

"Your abduction has nothing to do with your father's death," said the old man. "Your mother and Maria Luiz are to blame. They have lost their love and turned their back on our Lord God. They despise His person along with the Christian biblical God and, as a result, have injured others. Your mother and Maria Luiz will be here shortly, and, at this time, they will recant their sins and order will be restored," said John.

PJ rebutted, "John, or whatever your name is, when you refer to order, does this mean your understanding or interpretation of the order? Listen to yourself, you smell of hubris."

Taken aback, John said, "You may have a fundamental understanding of religious philosophy—albeit it is erroneous. How dare you question the order administered by my Lord God."

John struck PJ on the chin and as he was to strike again, PJ pulled the jackknife from his shoe. PJ thrust the knife into John's thigh; he struck bone.

John screamed for assistance from the guards outside the cell. As PJ removed the knife from John's thigh, he was about to cut his throat when the guards burst into the cell and threw PJ to the cement floor. They beat PJ repeatedly until he was unconscious. When PJ awoke, his hair was matted down with blood. He couldn't remember the last time he had tasted food or had a sip of water.

It had taken over 100 stitches to close John's wound. A quarter of an inch to the right and PJ could have sliced an artery, perhaps leading to the old man's death. As John placed the crutch in his armpit, he felt that he was able to walk.

John told the physician, "You had better go clean up the little bastard." John winced as he said, "We want the targets as calm as possible prior to their final confession."

Chapter 30

ALL THREE IN A ROW

On Tuesday, at precisely at 9:00 a.m., Samantha and Maria were at the entrance to the Vatican City Gardens. When they turned to proceed into the Gardens, they saw someone that resembled Sandra Wells. Samantha yelled, "Sandra…Sandra Wells!"

It was Sandra.

Sandra couldn't take her eyes off of Samantha. She had dark circles surrounding her eyes that were as red as desert clay. She was pale and looked terribly frail. It took all of Maria's support to make Samantha stand up straight.

Samantha said to Sandra, "They've taken PJ and I am frightened to death." She began to cry uncontrollably again. Samantha looked at Sandra and said "What…what are you doing here?"

Sandra said, "I am here to speak before the Catholic

Women for God. It was a hastily organized convention, and I was to be the primary speaker. Wait a second! All three of us together at the same time and same place—the odds are statistically impossible.

Sandra said, "I have been duped and you have been coerced into…"

Before Sandra could complete her thought, three men closed in behind them and thrust guns into their backs.

One of the men said, "We do not wish to harm you, but you must listen carefully. If you don't follow our instructions, we will kill you right here and furthermore, Ms. James, you will never see your son again. Carefully follow the priest in front of you. No sudden movements or loud sounds!"

They did as they were told. Samantha had little concern about a gun held to her back. She just wanted to hold PJ in her arms.

Stephen and Peter were amongst the crowds at the Vatican City Gardens; they saw the procession of the three women. They surreptitiously followed the three targets.

Chapter 31

SANDRA IN FLIGHT

On early Monday morning, Jack Wells was driving Sandra to the Salt Lake City International Airport. It wasn't a long drive—only four miles from downtown Salt Lake City. He knew it was a special tribute to her to be the guest speaker at the Catholic Women of God conference in the Vatican City. Sandra was uncharacteristically giddy.

Jack found it strange that they had provided her with only one day's notice. *But who cares?* She was happy, flying first class, and booked into a Marriot suite just outside the Vatican City.

It concerned him that he wouldn't see her for three days. Since the fire-bombing, they had been together every moment except when Sandra was at a church meeting or he was at the bureau. He held her tightly just before she received the first-class call to enter the plane.

Sandra had never flown first class. It was glorious! The

attendant in the first-class cabin offered her a small glass of champagne before takeoff. She would have customarily refused such an offer, but changed her mind and said, "Why thank you."

She wondered if she would tell Jack about the first and even second glass of champagne.

An older man sat next to her in the aisle seat. His willowy motions indicated that he was gay. He turned to her and said, "Hello, my name is Jonathan Laigo. This is my layover flight to Rome."

Jonathan Laigo was Winston Kelly's assumed name—one of many that he employed to stay one step ahead of the ever-present Federal agents.

Sandra introduced herself and said that she found herself lucky to be on a nonstop. Sandra continued, "I'm not an experienced flyer and I will have to apologize, in advance, if I grab your arm."

Kelly responded, "I have been fortunate enough to have flown around the world ten times over, but I still have a fear of flying. Luckily, we have four arms between us."

Sandra giggled and said, "Mr. Laigo…"

Winston Kelly immediately interrupted her and said, "Please call me John—everyone does."

Sandra continued, "So, John, what do you do for a living?"

Kelly responded, "I am an Associate Director of

Neuromorphic Studies at the University of Southern California. I deal mostly with a lot of high-tech nonsense." *No harm in telling at least a bit of truth*, he thought.

Sandra said, "I have a close friend who was a professor at USC. Her name is Samantha James. Do you know her?"

Bells and whistles went off in Kelly's head—he knew Samantha was, more or less, underground. "Samantha James... hmmm...I've heard the name but never met her."

"You would love her," said Sandra. "She is the sincerest person I have ever met. She also has looks to kill."

"Well, in that case," said Kelly, "I hope I have the pleasure of meeting her one day."

Sandra smiled and asked, "And what will you be doing in the lovely City of Rome?"

Unabashedly, Kelly responded, "I don't mind telling you that I am gay. The love of my life resides in Central America. We meet twice a year in Rome. It's a wonderful city for lovers."

Sandra just smiled and decided to have a third glass of champagne. By this time, she decided that she would tell Jack about her champagne consumption.

Kelly didn't realize that he was about to spend the time in Rome alone.

Two weeks prior, Charlie Wertz's home was surrounded by Federal agents in Belize. Rather than surrender his insight into the advanced neuromorphic chip, he committed suicide and burned any documents referencing "the chip." He was sorry he couldn't say goodbye to his lover Kelly or his neighbors, Samantha and Bobby.

Chapter 32

HOW FAR WILL THEY GO?

After he dropped Sandra off at the airport, Jack headed to the FBI building. When he walked in, he was surprised by the flurry of activity. This type of activity usually meant that an operation was in progress—a big one.

Seventeen members of the bureau were in meetings all day. Each of them wore a small black rose affixed to their suit coat. There were several rooms that read:

CONFIDENTIAL: BLACK ROSE ONLY.

Jack could hear the hum of keyboards and a number of hushed conversations.

Why wasn't he involved, he wondered. He knew he was one of the best field agents in the entire bureau.

Perhaps they had uncovered his involvement in the death of Diogenes and were preparing a case against him. Perhaps he was to be fired, or even worse, transferred to another field office.

It would break Sandra's heart if she was forced to leave Salt Lake City—this was the center of operations for the New Church of Lord God.

At 2:00 a.m. on Tuesday morning, the bureau office had been cleared out except for Jack. Since Sandra was travelling, he decided that he would work until his eyes could not absorb any additional punishment. He was investigating a plural marriage community in Northeast Utah. While a big operation seemed to be in progress, he was to direct his efforts to this nonsense. There were six male farmers and fourteen married women. The women were adamant in their desire to remain in their plural marriages.

"What the hell am I supposed to do?" asked Jack. "I don't believe in plural marriages, but if that's the way they want to live their lives, let them. Are we to storm the small village, guns a' blazing, to separate families? Let a lower pay grade agent take care of this dilemma."

As he turned his head to the right, he noticed that his sometimes-partner, Brian Lamley, had left a file on his desk. It was a strict policy at the Bureau that no files were to be left on one's desk once they left the office. Had Brian made a terrible oversight or was he trying to tell Jack something?

Jack moved to Brian's desk and saw a small black rose on top of a file labeled CONFIDENTIAL: BLACK ROSE ONLY. Jack opened the file to find a single piece of paper that had been redacted.

Jack carefully looked about the office to ensure that he was alone. The single sheet read:

BLACK ROSE PROJECT
(CONFIDENTIAL)

There are approximately 4_____, most of which are located in the _____ area of the United States. This is our _____.

The leader_____has caused a great deal of_____ in the_____ world._____expanding influence could result in_____. This_____ could also result in severe_____ consequences to the_____.

We intend by_____ night to_____ these +/- 45 _____. We would hope that there would be no civilians_____ in the_____. Nevertheless, if there are civilians in _____ they are to be considered collateral_____.

This operation will involve approximately_____ agents that operate in_____ cities.

By_____morning tomorrow, we will be placing_____ in the targets.

Tee time is 8 p.m. tomorrow. It is extremely important and no_____ or _____ are to be left behind.

This operation is of the utmost importance to_____
as well as_____. The survival of_____
may be at risk.

This operation must be a complete and total_____.

We understand that the leader of_____,
_____ is now or will shortly be in _____.

Our_____in this operation will be dealing
with_____.

Do not communicate with anyone about this operation unless
they can refer to or are wearing a black rose.

_____speed.

Director of the_____.

Jack's heart was racing; even though the document was
redacted, he knew that the New Church of Lord God, and,
more importantly, Sandra were the targets of the **Black Rose
Operation.**

He called Sandra's cell repeatedly. There was no answer
even when he posted the 911 request.

Jack was frozen in fear but he remembered Sandra's
warning, "If there is ever any trouble involving the New Church
of Lord God, call Stephen James, Samantha's father. He is
someone you can trust." Jack was at a loss—he didn't know who

to trust and, customarily, he would handle a situation like this by himself. This quandary was bigger than one man.

Jack awkwardly pulled Stephen James's phone number from his wallet.

Stephen reluctantly answered his cell and Jack introduced himself. Jack told Stephen of his suspicions surrounding the **Black Rose Operation** and his concerns for the safety of his wife, Sandra.

Stephen understood Jack's concern; the life of Samantha was also in jeopardy. As they talked through this enigma, Stephen said, "My group at this end have the perpetrators and the girls under observation. We are by no stretch of the imagination out of the woods but we're better off now than we were yesterday. Please don't alert any US authorities about Sandra's disappearance—they'll just get in our way and we may have to cross the lines."

Jack was comforted by the strength of Stephen's voice.

Stephen concluded the conversation by saying, "I hope I can call you with good news. But if you are a religious man, I would suggest that you resort to prayer. As to the US-based churches, I am sorry that you will have to be on your own. I have my hands full in the Vatican City. But, just a word of advice: don't bare your soul to anyone in Salt Lake City or the FBI. Go to a higher source." Stephen wished Jack good luck and then hung up.

***

Nole Pacis was the Solicitor General of the Department of Justice. He prided himself on the fact his office was just above the department's seal, Qui Pro Domina (Who Lady Justice Thrives). The placement of his office did not make up for the fact that he was dramatically underpaid.

Nole was a graduate of the Stanford Law School. He was the first in his graduating class. Despite this achievement, he was most proud of the football on his bookshelf; he had been honored with the game ball since he caught the touchdown pass that in the last second, let them beat the hated USC Trojans. His friend, Jack Wells, was the quarterback that threw the pass to him. Jack was ranked third in the graduating class. Nole would never let him live it down.

It was 5:30 in the morning when Nole's personal cell rang. He could see it was Jack. Nole answered, "What are you doing up at this time in the morning in Salt Lake? Are you about to congratulate me again for being ranked first in the law school class?"

He didn't elicit Jack's customary laugh. Something was awry.

Jack responded, "I need the DOJ's assistance and I need it fast!"

"Of course, Jack—anything that is humanly possible," offered Nole.

"Something's going on in the Salt Lake City Bureau. As

you know, Sandra has become the leader of a huggy-type church known as the New Church of Lord God," said Jack.

"Oh yes, I read about it in *Time Magazine*—quite the controversy. I would be more interested if I wasn't an atheist," replied Nole.

Jack quickly responded, "This new church has pissed off a lot of people—especially the Mormons. Surprisingly, Sandra's church continues to grow while the Mormon pews seem to be diminishing. With decreasing numbers in the pews, tithes have reduced, and you know how the Mormons feel about money."

"So, what does this David versus Goliath religious battle have to do with the DOJ?" asked Nole.

"Cut out the cute comments; this is serious stuff," said Jack. I found a confidential paper in the Salt Lake City bureau, labeled as the **Black Rose Operation**.

"Nole, listen to me,' Jack said emphatically. "Within approximately 30 hours, the **Black Rose Operation,** spearheaded by the Salt Lake City Bureau, is going to blast the 47 churches to hell. They aren't worried about anyone in the church—if there are innocents killed in the blasts, they are simply to be labeled as collateral damage. You are my only hope. I can't contact anyone in the bureau, for several offices are involved in this operation."

"Jack, have you been drinking?" pressed Nole. "This is preposterous."

"Nole, just check out two of the churches for explosive devices as a favor to me," Jack replied. "If you find devices in this small sample, they'll be in every church. If you don't do something fast, Nole, you're going to have a whole lot of burned churches and maybe some collateral damage. You've got to believe me, Nole."

"Ok, Ok, Jack," said Nole. "I'll see what I can find out. If I put my teams on it, we can be lightning fast, but if this story is an illusion, I'll be out of the DOJ and practicing family law in some goddamned place like Fresno."

Six hours later, Nole called Jack's cell. Jack had stepped out of the bureau office to speak with Nole. Even then Jack spoke in hushed tones.

"Jack, you may have something—eight of the churches we searched are set up with enough plastics to replicate a small thermonuclear device. The explosions were not to be contemporaneous. Some were set for six o'clock, a couple for seven o'clock and the rest for eight o'clock. The guys that set these explosives up knew what they were doing..."

Jack interrupted: "The FBI has always had experts in this field."

Just around six o'clock, Nole called again. "I just wanted to let you know that we have rounded up over 90 agents involved in the **Black Rose Operation**. I can't believe it! We have also placed the President of the Church of Jesus Christ of Latter Day Saints, Russell Newton, under arrest. But as you can imagine, he was out on a $5 million bail in a flash. There is some conjecture that another religious organization is somehow involved but we haven't got that far yet. I've saved the worst for last, though," said Nole.

Jack held his breath as he expected to hear of Sandra's death.

Nole continued, "We couldn't get to one church in time. The timer was set for four o'clock. The blast occurred during an arts and crafts class in a Maine church. Thirty-six children were burned to death."

How far will organized religion go in its quest...? thought Jack to himself.

Jack was still waiting for a call from Stephen James as he pondered the seriousness of the situation.

Chapter 33

ENTERING THE NECROPOLIS

The Vatican Necropolis is between sixteen and thirty feet below Saint Peter's Basilica. It is a collection of mausoleums in which multiple tombs have been enshrined. The mausoleums are labeled A–Z and Psi. The most renowned remains in the Necropolis are those of the Apostle Peter who was martyred in the year 64 in the circus of Nero. Nero conveniently had Peter crucified upside down and buried in a single rock tomb in that very Necropolis.

The Necropolis has been subject to a significant number of excavations for over eighty years. The excavations began in 1940 under the direction of Pope Pius XI—for prideful in all respects, it was his desire to be buried as close as possible to Peter the Apostle.

This particular Tuesday and Wednesday, the Vatican Necropolis was closed to visitors; apparently a number of technical touch-ups needed to be made.

Bobby had rented a ten-passenger helicopter so they would have direct access to the Vatican City and, if they were successful, an expedient means of escape would be available. Stephen, Bobby, and Peter landed in the only aviation facility in the Vatican City—the Vatican City Heliport. They were dressed much like the more than 2,400 lay workers that served as the Vatican City workforce. They had paid a small fortune for insignias and special passes, indicating that they were high-tech engineers. As such, they were permitted unlimited access to all areas of the Vatican City during the course of the restoration work.

Peter noticed that the entrances to the Necropolis were surrounded by Pontifical Swiss Guards. Since the Vatican City had no armed forces, it was the responsibility of the Swiss Guard to act as security for the Pope and other high-ranking religious officials.

It seemed odd to Peter that approximately 70 guards were attached to the entrances since the Swiss Guard only had 150 members. Employing nearly half of the Guard seemed like overkill for restoration work.

Peter found a deserted area in the Vatican Gardens. He looked to Stephen and Bobby and said, "As you know, we are working on a short fuse with respect to the location and recovery of Samantha, PJ, Maria, and Sandra. As a word of warning, don't be fooled by the size of the Vatican City. It's only 110 acres, of which 57 are represented by these gardens. Nevertheless, there are numerous places to sequester four hostages.

"Furthermore, don't be fooled by its small population of 1,000. On any given day, even with the closure of the Necropolis, over 50,000 people could be sightseeing in Saint Peter's Basilica, the Sistine Chapel, and the various Vatican museums." Peter continued. "I am convinced that the former Pope John is behind this conspiracy. He doesn't like to lose.

"It's 11:00 a.m. now and we already saw the three girls being led into the Vatican Gardens. I would bet that their captors will eventually turn left into the Necropolis and meet up with PJ.

"In the past, the Pope and I, along with various ancillary personnel, have been in countless crevices and openings in the Necropolis that are hidden to public eyes. I am not proud of the special dispensations that occurred in those sites, but they do provide me with a working knowledge as to where the four could be held.

"John is a very methodical man," Peter added. "I would imagine that we have between twelve and twenty-four hours before he can orchestrate confessions and plan for the dispensation of the four. Within that time span, I would hope that we could extricate the four and reach the heliport. I would propose that we enter the Necropolis at dusk."

Stephen was angered. "Twelve to twenty-four hours is a large time grid," he said. They could be inside being tortured and near death as we speak. My vote is to proceed immediately. And, by the way, this is not some goddamned sterile operation in Pakistan. They do have names—they are not 'the four!'"

"I apologize," said Peter, "and I understand your anxiety. Samantha and PJ are just as important to me as they are to you. But to rush our targeted sites in open daylight with seventy Swiss Guards in our face would be suicide and may lead to an early demise of our loved ones." Peter was careful not to use the term "the four."

Stephen seemed to be satisfied.

Peter continued, "I just want to be sure that they have not doubled back into the Apostolic Palace. The Palace holds just as many disguised leeways as does the Necropolis. I believe I have an ally in the Palace with Father McNally. He was once the president of the Pontifical Commission. This Commission was organized to administer all the legislative functions of the Vatican City and often was in conflict with Pope John. Father McNally knew of John's multiple schemes that were tainted by corruption and depravity and despised him for it. Let's hope he is still alive—maybe he can provide us with some additional insight."

As they approached the Palace, they were stopped by three

of the elite Swiss Guards. Peter spoke to them in Latin and revealed their special passes. They were readily granted access to the Palace.

Peter led Stephen and Bobby upstairs to an office on the second floor. He knocked quietly and heard a feeble voice say, "Enter."

Father McNally was clearly elderly; his skin hung in disgust to his slight frame.

"My Lord!" cried McNally. "I thought you were dead, Peter."

"Pope John tried his best to kill me. But you know me, Father McNally—I was always very lucky." said Peter.

"What are you doing here?" inquired Father McNally. "If they find you this time, they will most certainly succeed in their desire to eliminate you." McNally paid no attention to either Stephen or Bobby.

"Father McNally," said Peter, "I believe our beloved former Pope is devising a heinous scheme that will probably lead to the death of four innocent people that have been kidnapped and brought to the Vatican City. With false confessions and the eventual death of the innocents, he must believe that he can restore his credibility within Mother Church. The innocents, in part, are associated with the manuscript discovery and dissemination of a highly controversial manuscript. I am sure you have read about the Qumran Cave 12 saga."

"Oh yes, I have followed the saga quite carefully but I am from the old school and I am not entirely convinced about this philosophy of a woman Lord God. Despite my feelings, however, you know I have never trusted that bastard John. At best, he embodies everything that is evil. What can I do to help?" asked McNally.

"Father McNally, have you noticed anything peculiar this morning—is it possible that our friends and family could be here in the palace?" said Peter.

"They are not here," said Father McNally. "I know every movement and action that occurs in the Palace. But as an old man, I do little but stare out the window. I did notice there has been considerable activity recently outside the Palace." McNally excused himself as he coughed up phlegm from his ancient lungs.

"As I said, there has been considerable activity at the entrances to the Necropolis—particularly in the B–R areas. I know it's not much, but it's all I know," said McNally.

Peter thanked Father McNally and accompanied Stephen and Bobby as they proceeded cautiously to the Necropolis. They waited until right after dark to enter.

Peter then said to Stephen and Bobby, "You two take the front entrance and search areas H through Q. I'll go in the back way and take Psi through R. Listen for quiet voices, then gently tap on the walls to see if they are fabricated—there may be hidden rooms in the rear. Anytime you see a crucifix that is hand-painted on the wall, more likely than not there is a hidden door nearby. Finally, if you see any newly installed electrical wire, cut it. John might be just insane enough to set off explosions that could implode the entire Necropolis even if it means his own death. Good luck and Godspeed."

Just before he entered the front entrance to the Necropolis, Stephen called Jack Wells. "Jack, we are going into the Necropolis. If we succeed, I will need you to arrange a transport out."

Chapter 34

CAVE - IN

S amantha, Maria, and Sandra were tied to chairs in a
Necropolis cell. They were in the P area, for the former Pope
thought it would be appropriate for them to perish in Saint
Peter's grave site. A single Swiss Guard stood at attention in
front of them. The cell door was ajar as the guard was waiting
for John to arrive—besides, the three women weren't going
anywhere.

Samantha looked around the dingy enclosure. It was ten by
fourteen feet and had a small light. In the back of the room was
a small alcove covered overhead by a set of bars. She thought she
could smell fresh air emanating from the alcove.

The Swiss Guard was attacked by a fit of sneezing—
probably caused by dust. Maria carefully handed over an
instrument behind her back to Samantha during the course of
his sneezing bout. Maria had already untied Sandra's hands.

Samantha screamed in terror as she saw the former Pope
leading PJ into the cell. PJ's face was swollen, black and blue,

and his eyes were nearly closed. John was limping and placed PJ in a chair next to Samantha. He loosely tied PJ to the chair.

"You bastard!" screamed Samantha. "Is this how you treat children?"

"Don't worry, Mom," said PJ. "I nearly took his leg off. We were having an argument about his religious dogma. I won the argument!"

John disregarded PJ's comment.

John continued calmly, "I am bringing in a priest to hear your final confessions—except for you, Mrs. Wells, for you have not received a proper baptism."

"Don't bother," said Samantha. "We have no sins to confess."

"As you wish," said John, "but without final absolution, you know your next stop will be purgatory."

Out of the corner of his eye, PJ caught his mother slowly and quietly tearing at the ropes behind her back. PJ thought, *Stall, I've got to stall!*

"No final absolution and then straight to purgatory? That's another piece of your religious bullshit," said PJ. "It's people like you that permanently removed the six pages of the Gospel of Mary from its beginning and four pages from its middle. Did you ever wonder what they might have revealed?"

"It matters little to me, for Saint Peter said that Jesus would not have revealed important teachings to a woman and her stature cannot be greater than that of male apostles," proclaimed John.

Samantha looked to PJ and said to herself, *Please keep him talking just a little bit more.*

Samantha said to PJ, "You might remind this reprehensible former pope about Levi."

John dismissed the Swiss Guard and told him that Father Timothy was not required to provide a final absolution for any of the hostages.

PJ continued, "Have you forgotten that Levi, in defense of Mary, told Saint Peter that surely the Savior loved her more than all of his apostles?"

John responded, "You do not know the body of our religion. You only select pieces that will support your heresy."

Peter was weaving through the Necropolis. He had severed a number of the newly installed electrical wires. As he approached area P, he heard voices. He picked up his pace.

"Shut up old man," said Samantha. "You know nothing of the true Lord God." She bolted from her chair, apple corer in hand. Maria never went anywhere without her apple corer.

In a single motion, Samantha thrust the apple corer through the Pope's eye and into his brain. As he fell to the ground, he pressed a small device that was attached to his hip.

There was an explosion as Peter rushed into the cell. He thought he had severed all of the electrical wires. "Dammit, I must have missed one," said Peter.

As the cave began to crumble, Peter quickly hurled Samantha, PJ, Maria, and Sandra into the alcove.

Peter and the former pope were instantly covered by tons of rock and earth. Samantha and the group were partially protected by the bars above the alcove but were still enveloped by the same rock and earth.

Suddenly, it was quiet.

Samantha struggled to breathe and a white glow appeared in her consciousness. PJ and Sandra passed through the white glow. *Is this how one dies slowly?* she thought.

Samantha, faintly, heard her father's voice. Maria and her father were pulling her body from the rubble.

Samantha screamed, "Get PJ out!"

They rushed as quickly as possible out of the Necropolis to the heliport and then to the international airport where a US Air Force cargo plane awaited them. Jack Wells was the smiling pilot.

Chapter 35

SISTERS

The loss of Peter was still there. He was clasped in her mind every minute of the day. As PJ registered in a private school in Tulsa, Samantha and Maria once again began to walk through the apple grove. They also began to speak of girly things as they had in the past and occasionally giggled. Sometimes Sandra would fly in from Salt Lake City to join them.

Two years after Peter's death, Samantha and Maria, on an Easter Sunday, decided to walk to the farthest reaches of the apple grove.

There She was, on her knees, tending to a sickly and frail-looking apple tree. She looked to Maria and said, "You have really got to fertilize the trees more often, especially the weaker ones."

Maria nodded but said nothing.

"As for you, Samantha, you are becoming a pain in my ass," said the Lord God. "If it isn't one thing with you, it's another. I can't spend an inordinate amount of time with a single being, for there are billions of others that require care on earth like the sick apple tree. Multiply that by billions of planets in the universe and you will understand my dilemma."

"I do understand and am sincerely sorry," said Samantha.

Almost ashamed, the Lord God smiled at Samantha and said, "I apologize. Please don't listen to my ranting. I just get a little grumpy around this time of the year. It brings back memories of my one and only Son."

She quickly changed the subject and said, "Samantha, you are lucky my sister was with you at the Necropolis."

Shocked, Samantha said, "Sister?"

"Yes," she said. "Maria is just as much a Lord God as I am. She is just taking a small respite. Maria provides me a bit of reverence only because I am, unfortunately, the eldest.

"I apologize for the ruse," the Lord God explained, "but I needed Maria as close to you as possible. Your message will someday change the entire world. I have spent a great deal of time and energy on my children in this world," she added. "Besides my sincere love for these children, I have also cried oceans of tears with their tragedies. I couldn't bear to see all of my children vaporized by computer singularity.

"I must warn you, as did Charlie Wertz, of the dangers of an artificial intelligence that can be inserted into a computer—a computer that, if left unmonitored, could achieve such singularity.

"Neither Maria nor I can aid humankind when it violates the parameters of free will: mass shootings in schools, temples, or mosques, the abuse of children and the elderly, thefts of money and property, and the molestations that preceded the Me Too movement, et cetera, et cetera, et cetera. All of this could have and should have been avoided. Singularity fits in this league and you should be able to avert it. Humankind is not stupid, but sometimes is just plain lazy when it comes to solving problems, large or small.

"The human race created the computer, the neuromorphic chip, and the beginnings of artificial intelligence. If they created it, they should be able to control it.

"Samantha, you are a smart lady. Maybe you could assist in addressing this singularity issue. PJ may also be able to help you. He will eventually become a renowned cybernetics professor and, in deference to your father, he will also become a part-time Episcopal priest."

Samantha made a face.

The Lord God remarked, "Oh, cut it out, Samantha. You know Episcopal priests can marry and you can have a bunch of grandchildren."

Suddenly, the sky darkened and She began to walk away. She stopped to turn around and face Samantha. "Maria is probably too shy to tell you but she doesn't like Lennon's and

McCartney's music. She is a rabid fan, however, of Julio Iglesias. I find him too syrupy, but she is my baby sister and she can have whatever she wants."

Maria smiled. Not long after, the mainstay in music at the Bar SB Ranch became Julio Iglesias.

Maria and Rodriguez were ecstatic.

Chapter 36

MARIA'S EMPOWERMENT

Maria disappeared one day amongst the apple trees on an early fall day at the Wilkinson Ranch. Typically, Samantha would accompany her in a near-twilight stroll through the grove. On this particular day, Maria insisted on being alone. As Maria walked out the door, she hugged Samantha and kissed her on the forehead. Maria had never acted so emotionally. Samantha felt it was time.

When Maria didn't return, Samantha found Rodriguez and they searched the apple grove all night and through the next day. They never discovered Maria's body or any evidence of violence.

Rodriguez instinctively felt it was the Lord God's way. Samantha and Rodriguez cried for days on end after Maria's disappearance. Rodriguez stopped communicating.

While sifting through her purse to find the keys to her old Ford F-250, Samantha found a letter addressed to her that was marked as personal and confidential. It was in Maria's handwriting. She opened the letter which read:

Dear Samantha:

Except for my sister, I had never had a true friend until I met you. What fun we had on our walks and the things we would say to each other still make me blush.

It is my time to go. It was my decision—not my sister's. I could see the tension in her eyes. It's too big of a job for just one.

I have never told Rodriguez or my children who I really am. I would prefer to keep it this way. Although, I have always felt that Rodriguez had a strange suspicion. If at all possible, could you please keep an eye on the children and especially Rodriguez? The children have husbands and children of their own but Rodriguez, after 60 years of marriage, has no one to comfort him.

I will love you always and maybe someday we can meet in the ranch's apple grove.

Take good care of my keepsake—the apple corer. It's in the second drawer in the kitchen cabinet, right next to the silverware. It always had provided me with a sense of empowerment and it might provide you with the same.

Love, Always and Forever,
Maria

Although reticent, Samantha arranged for a service at the tiny Catholic Church just outside of the city limits. It was a small service, including Samantha's family and Maria's daughters, their families, and Rodriguez. Rodriguez said nothing during the service. He simply maintained a steadfast but blank stare. Samantha, amidst her tears, was falling into a rabbit hole surrounded by depression.

Seeing the depth of her grief, her father took Samantha aside and held her closely. "Samantha," he said softly, "after telling me of the meeting with the Sisters, you must realize that you have been singled out. You are blessed. She has surrounded you with people who have aided in protecting you: Professor el-Zebn, Peter, Maria and, in a strange way, Charlie Wertz.

"Don't discount their actions. In one way or another they have protected both your life and that of PJ. This is not a time for self-pity or tears. This is a time for you to dig deep to find an inner strength. You must snap out of it: I didn't raise you to surrender. I love you, Sam," he assured her.

Bobby found Rodriguez in his beloved truck, the music playing a somber piece by Julio Iglesias. Rodriguez had died two weeks after the disappearance of Maria. Since he been eight years old, Rodriguez wore a simple chain crucifix around his neck. He trusted that it was an expression of his love for Maria.

Samantha removed Rodriguez's crucifix from his neck and gathered Maria's apple corer and her ring that Peter once held. She found a safe place in her purse for the precious mementos.

She felt as though each of them provided her with an inner sense of strength.

The purse never left her side.

Chapter 37

JAKE AND THE NORMAL COURSE OF THINGS

Jake was recently elected mayor of Wilkinson. The people of Wilkinson felt that although he was a recent arrival, he was perfectly fit for the job—intelligent and straight-talking. Most importantly, he was the only candidate running for the office.

He never introduced himself by employing a surname. He was simply "Jake."

Jake was fifty-ish, good-looking, and wealthy. As the founder and CEO of a San Mateo software development and primary chip firm, he wanted to get away from the traffic, the noise, and the aggressive bands of those who had been reduced to poverty. His brother had told him of the paradise that existed in Wilkinson, Oklahoma. Jake believed him.

Jake had met Samantha at the post office one Saturday morning. Jake was struck by her middle-aged beauty and by her Ford F-250.

"Hello, I'm Jake," he said, as he extended an open hand to Samantha.

"Nice to meet you, Jake, I'm Samantha," she said as she offered him a firm handshake in return.

Jake said, "I'll bet my old Ford 150 has more dents than yours."

As she turned to leave, Samantha said with a sly grin, "Maybe so, but mine is bigger than yours."

Samantha had driven past Jake's 5,000 acre ranch several times and wondered, *What did he have to hide? Everyone in Wilkinson has something to hide.*

Jake knew Samantha would be at the post office at exactly 11:30 a.m. every Saturday. Jake made sure he was, accidentally, there the same time.

PJ was home from school during the summer break. He couldn't spend a great deal of time at the ranch, but since he was now a full professor, he had a couple of weeks to spare.

Accompanying his mother to the post office, PJ instantly spotted Jake.

"I apologize," said PJ, "but aren't you…"

Jake shook PJ's hand and responded, "Just call me Jake."

"It's a pleasure, Jake. My name is Paul James and my mother doesn't know it, but she made a small fortune on Cyber Tech's initial public offering. More importantly, I have read all of your textbooks and I use the most recent one in my graduate studies class at USC."

Jake was red-faced and obviously embarrassed. He said, "With the recent advancements in cybernetics, I'm afraid my textbooks will soon become ancient history. Furthermore, I have read all of your published papers. They are brilliant and are clearly proof of the fact that you are light years ahead of me when dealing with cybernetics and chip development."

It was PJ's turn to be red-faced as he said, "You are too kind, Jake." PJ continued, "Why don't you come over for dinner tonight? Maybe we can talk a little shop. My students will be amazed when they discover that I had a chance to talk with you face-to-face."

"Don't you think we should ask your mother first?" Jake asked.

With a devilish smile, Samantha said, "How can I refuse your point-counterpoint as to who has the greater sense of hero worship?"

Both Jake and PJ, concurrently, blushed.

"How about 8:00 p.m.?" asked Samantha. "The three of us can have a little Scotch and then some dinner. Don't expect anything special for dinner—I flunked homemaking in high school."

"So did I," said Jake. "Nevertheless, I'll bring the Scotch. Do you prefer J&B, Johnny Walker Blue, or Johnny Walker Black?"

"Black!" said Samantha with emphasis.

After dinner, Samantha sat by the fire and read while PJ and Jake discussed esoteric concepts revolving around cybernetics, chips, and computers. They were enjoying themselves.

Samantha thought to herself, *Is it possible that I gave birth to a nerd? A cuddly bear, but still a nerd?*

Without asking, PJ invited Jake to dinner most every night until he had to return to the USC campus. Samantha thought it strange that they sometimes would speak in somber tones.

The day before PJ was to return to school, PJ asked his mother if he could be excused and have dinner with Jake. PJ said, "He wants to introduce me to his brother. Jake claims he is a computer genius. He also asked me to invite you, though I think you'll just be terribly bored," said PJ.

"Sometimes boredom isn't so bad," said Samantha, "so count me in," she insisted.

As she entered Jake's house, Samantha felt a bit of house envy. It had a large fountain in the foyer and was elegantly designed with priceless artwork and furnishings— right out of The Architectural Digest.

"Your home is exquisite. Who was your designer?" asked Samantha.

"It was my very talented brother," replied Jake. "Not only is he an excellent designer, but he is also probably the brightest computer development specialist and cybernetic theorist in the world," Jake said with pride.

Winston Kelly raced out of the kitchen with a plate of hors d'oeuvres. He saw Samantha and dropped the plate to the floor. The fine china broke into a hundred pieces.

"You are still as beautiful as ever, Sam—maybe even more so," said Winston. They hugged as Winston began to cry. "You know they caused Charlie's suicide," said Winston. "I am still not over it. They have no idea who they are dealing with."

Inadvertently, Winston removed his hand from his shirt pocket and something fell to the floor.

Winston picked up the fragment and said, "This was our most recently developed neuromorphic chip. It could be topically implanted, with ease, using something equivalent to a small staple gun. The recipient would hardly be aware of the chipping—he might only sense something like a small bug bite. One day I will exact my revenge."

PJ and Jake examined the chip carefully. Jake, noticing a small CW insignia on the corner, wondered why his brother would keep such a valuable discovery in a shirt pocket.

Winston, still sobbing, stuttered and said, "I will keep this near to me in memory of Charlie." Winston turned to PJ and said, "Samantha, this must be PJ. He has turned into a magnificent specimen."

Samantha raised her eyebrow just enough to let Winston know that he might have crossed the line.

Jake stared at Samantha and she thought to herself, *Just Plain Jake was actually Jake Kelly, Winston's brother. Winston was the reason Jake needed to hide in Wilkinson.*

"Sam," said Winston, "I see that you have met my brother Jackson. We call him Jake. Isn't he a doll?" asked Winston.

Jake gave Winston a stern but brotherly look.

Winston continued, "Sam, I have been in Wilkinson for nearly three months. I wanted to contact you earlier but it has been just too dangerous."

PJ interjected, "Mom, I am not sure you should be here. We are going to be discussing some things that may be, at best, delicate."

Jake chimed in, "PJ may be right, Samantha. The world is generally better off if we just let things assume their natural course. PJ, Winston, and I have decided we may have to alter this natural course."

Samantha looked to Jake and said, "My life has been beset by a number of life-changing events. If Winston and my son feel that the normal course of operations in the world must be changed, then I might be a valuable asset."

"Even if it could involve the loss of your life?" asked Jake.

"Even if," replied Samantha.

Beguiled, Jake thought to himself, *This woman has some mettle about her.*

Chapter 38

THE MARK OF THE BEAST AND SINGULARITY

In the early twenty-first century, mankind began to experiment with chipping. A grain-sized chip would initially be implanted in-between the thumb and forefinger. The implants were barely noticeable and, for all practical purposes, turned the human species into walking smart cards. Doors could be opened, computers could be unlocked, purchases could be made, and emails could be sent or received without any human interaction.

The chips could also serve as GPS tracking devices which would monitor latitude, longitude, altitude, speed, direction, or movement of the embedded receptor. This GPS tracking chip was comparable to the one embedded in PJs hand by Winston Kelly right after his birth.

Winston Kelly and Charles Wertz turned the world of chip technology upside down when they developed an advanced neuromorphic chip in the mid-twenty-first century. This chip, when placed amidst the neurons and synapses in the human brain, could possibly regulate human behavior.

Charlie was not a religious man but he wondered if this chip was more capricious than the "Mark of the Beast," as foretold in the Book of Revelation. Beyond the potential to alter human behavior, the neuromorphic chip also had long-term implications as to the very survival of the human species.

As Charlie had once explained to Bobby James, when inserted into a supercomputer, the chip could lead to an artificial intelligence that would allow the computer to create a better version of itself over and over again.

This duplication process could eventually result in the supercomputer's ability to achieve singularity—a point at which the computer would become smarter than humans. In reaching singularity, the supercomputers, left unmonitored, could spin out of control and dramatically modify human civilization. Charlie envisioned an environment where the supercomputers would consider the human species a petulant irritant that could easily be eradicated.

This was the foundation for the Lord God's warning to Samantha.

Although frightening, the advanced neuromorphic chip was a labor of love. Winston and Charlie had spent nearly five years in its development. No one was aware of its discovery—not even Jake Kelly, Winston's brother.

During the course of the chip's development, Charlie and Winston would continue their work throughout the night. Evan Wakefield, the manager of the Jet Stream Cleaning crew, wondered why he would often find his friends asleep at their desks. Sometimes, he would cover them with clean, Jet Stream Cleaning uniforms.

Chapter 39

THE TWO BOYS PLUS ONE

Winston Kelly, Jake Kelly, and Hugh Stapleton grew up in Corona Del Mar, California. Winston was four years older than Jake and Hugh and often spent his time alone—he was different. Jake and Hugh were attached at the hip while growing up.

Jake and Hugh, at one time or another, had just about every pretty girl at Corona Del Mar High in the back seat of their cars. It was a competition and they would tell each other heated tales as to how they had convinced the young girls to take off their bras and panties. It was the best of times for them—surfing in the morning amidst the great whites, then hurrying to school and waiting for the weekend parties.

Jake applied to USC and was easily accepted. Stapleton made his way into USC after his father made a visit to the business office to make a substantial contribution to the USC

Annual Fund in exchange for Hugh's acceptance into the freshman class.

While at USC, Jake would often be found in the stacks of the Hancock Library, stowing away to study cybernetics and computer theory. He had a second major in entrepreneurial studies. He wanted to make money and lots of it.

Stapleton would occasionally delve into books, but he was more interested in campus politics. With the aid of Theta Nu Epsilon (TNE), the university's clandestine political fraternity, Hugh became the school's president. Any candidate that was backed by TNE never lost an election. The members of TNE were dead serious and several of its members had, over the course of a number of years, infiltrated the highest levels of American politics.

Despite their varied paths, they spoke frequently on the phone and whenever possible would meet to see who could consume the most J&B Scotch. Each was successful in his own quarter.

Jake was in his heart an entrepreneur and started a software development and microchip firm called Cyber Technology. The firm was immensely successful and eventually he took the company public. Before long, he was a billionaire. For fun, Jake began to write computer/cybernetic textbooks. They were well received and even his genius brother, Winston, used the textbooks in his graduate school classes.

Stapleton, after graduating from law school, worked for the law firm of Evans and Yucca, a high-powered law firm that served as counsel for a number of extremely visible political figures. By thirty-four, he was the managing partner of the firm. In 2046, a Congressional seat had become vacant in Orange County, California. Stapleton ran and won convincingly. He was a perfect fit—young, well spoken, good looking, and a fiscal conservative with a heart. It was impossible to dislike him.

With Hugh's continued success in Congress, he ran for the presidency. Stapleton won the election, and in 2056 became the 54th president of the United States.

Winston Kelly wasn't as odd as everyone thought since he met Charles Wertz at a cybernetics lab at USC. They became immediate lovers and shared a genuine like talent in the field of neuromorphic studies.

While in graduate school and employing the Freedom of Information Act, they stumbled upon documents surrounding the CIA's controversial Project Artichoke.

Project Artichoke posed a diabolical question: *Are we able to gather sufficient control over an individual to have him or her do our bidding even if it violates fundamental values—fundamental values including self-preservation?* The CIA hypothesized that a silent weapon could inflict as much damage as a traditional form of weaponry.

They envisioned that a bio-engineered implant might induce the human brain to accept and act upon designated agendas. The CIA's grandiose plans even conceived that designated frequencies could be disseminated amongst large populations—frequencies that could incite agitation, anxiety, and aggression.

The concept of mind control scared the crap out of Winston and Charles and it was never their intent to follow such a path of study.

It came by accident, for with the development of the neuromorphic chip, they confirmed the underlying theory advanced by Project Artichoke. With the discovery of the neuromorphic chip, Winston and Charles secluded themselves.

They had made a colossal discovery—one that was too dangerous to make public. Despite the implications of such a dangerous proposition, they had promised each other that they would be partners for life.

Chapter 40

TERROR IN THE WHITE HOUSE

S tapleton's vice president was Daniel Mullen, a Harvard graduate. Mullen was a brilliant technician and a scientist. He had a minor degree in computer studies and was always studying new developments in the computer field.

These developments were more than a hobby for Mullen— they were an obsession. He would often express his concerns to Stapleton, especially those involving the recent but clandestine advances in the computer industry. He would often discuss the theory of unbridled *singularity* and its potential draconian consequences. Stapleton was a good listener and, although he was not an alarmist, he initiated a congressional study into the issue of *singularity*. The committee was headed by Mullen and two members of the House.

The lengthy study by the investigative committee was to be presented on the House floor in an open forum on Thursday afternoon.

On Wednesday night Mullen, the chair and the vice chair of the Investigative Committee, respectively Anna Lee Obama (the granddaughter of the former president) and Symington Abraham (the current Speaker of the House) met in a small room in the Capitol. They were in the midst of preparing their agenda for the open-air forum involving *singularity* and, more importantly, the implications if it were to become unrestrained. They knew it was going to be an uphill battle. Most of the current Congress couldn't spell *singularity*.

It was 2:30 in the morning when they called downstairs for the delivery of an everything pizza. It wasn't necessarily a healthy menu, but it would stave off the lingering hunger pangs of the members.

Within twenty minutes, there was a tap at the door.

"Finally," said Anna Lee Obama. "I'm starved."

Mullen answered the door and said in a surprised voice, "Hello, Brian…"

Before he could continue, Brian slit Mullen's throat from ear to ear. The assassin, with lightning speed, offered Obama and Abraham the same. There were pools of blood everywhere.

The assassin quickly removed the bloodied Jet Stream Cleaning uniform and threw it, along with his knife, into a black plastic bag.

Moments later, there was a knock at the door. It was the

butler from downstairs delivering the pizza. As the assassin opened the door slightly, the butler screamed in terror. He could see bodies amidst the massive amounts of blood.

The butler dropped the pizza and ran down the adjoining corridor.

The assassin had no choice—he had to use his Berretta. He opened up on the butler, killing him instantaneously. The sound from the gun reverberated throughout the Capitol halls and suddenly security was everywhere. He looked to the left and found an open maintenance closet. He carefully opened it, slid in, and locked it from the inside. He held his breath and was accompanied only by his rapid heartbeat.

Richard Smith, the head of Capitol security, traced bloodied footprints outside the room that held the victims to the small maintenance room. He turned the doorknob—it was locked. He screamed, "Come out with your hands up or I will empty my chamber into the door—and I mean do it now!"

As the assassin opened the door, Smith said, "What are you doing in this closet, Senator Orin?"

The senator said nothing and placed a single bullet into Smith's head. He was dead before he hit the floor. Orin knew there were too many of them, so he put the Berretta under his chin and pulled the trigger.

Chapter 41

LOCKDOWN

Jake's phone rang at 4:30 a.m. on Thursday. He could see that it was a 911 call from Hugh Stapleton. With a sense of urgency, Jake picked up his cell and said, "It's too early for good news, Hugh. What's the matter?"

Hugh, in a curious but stern voice said, "Jake, I need you back here right away. The senior senator from Utah, Brian Orin, killed the vice president and two prominent congressmen early this morning. It's a conundrum in a box within a puzzle. Orin was well respected on the Hill, had a lovely family, and was expected to run for the Presidency after the end of my term.

"I have his cadaver in lockdown until we can piece together some quantifiable facts. The only thing that is abundantly clear is that the autopsy revealed a small chip in his head. My jet will meet you at the Tulsa International Airport."

***

Hugh didn't expect a party of four, but he knew that Jake must have had his reasons.

Jake hugged Hugh and proceeded to introduce his team.

"Hugh, you already know my brother, Winston. Winston is clearly the most renowned specialist in the field of neuromorphic studies in the world. He recently revealed to me that he, along with his associate Charles Wertz, developed a neuromorphic chip—a chip that, if planted into a human brain, could alter the recipient's behavior."

Hugh found this statement uncomfortably familiar and it sent chills down his spine.

Jake continued, "Next to Winston is Paul James, a brilliant young professor of cybernetics and computer studies. And, of course, you know Samantha James. I believe you presented her with the Presidential Medal of Freedom last year."

Samantha extended her hand to greet the President. Hugh disregarded her hand and caressed her in a longing hug. It was too long and the hair on the back of Jake's neck began to bristle.

"Sam, I am so happy to see you again," said the President.

"Hugh," said Jake, "you must know Sam a great deal better than I expected."

"Oh, it's nothing," said Hugh. "We simply had dinner a couple of times prior to the Medal of Freedom ceremonies."

Jake knew that look in Hugh's eyes—it was the same one he displayed at Corona Del Mar High School.

Jake stepped forward and said, "Samantha is here because,

as you must know, she has a storied past and may be the most capable of all of us. She clearly has an angel on her shoulder."

Close, but not exactly, thought Samantha.

"Hugh," Jake said, "I am the least credentialed of the group and am probably just along for the ride."

"Whether for the ride or not," said Hugh, "I need you here. Your judgment is impeccable and you have an uncanny ability to create solutions where there is a minefield of problems." Hugh knew how to polish the pride of his longtime friend.

"Let's go to the morgue," said the President. "I want you to take a close look at the body of Senator Orin."

As they entered the morgue, Senator Orin was lying on a steel table. Half of his head had been blown off.

The room was enveloped with the smell of death and formaldehyde. Thrown across the lower part of his body was a bloodied Jet Stream Cleaning uniform.

Jake, Winston, and PJ approached the body and began to carefully survey the corpse. PJ was the first to detect the remains of a small Band-Aid hanging from the left side of the skull. Under the Band-Aid was a small chip.

PJ turned to Winston and asked, "Is it a neuromorphic chip?"

Winston picked up a pair of small tweezers from the table and carefully removed the chip. He examined it methodically and said, "It's unquestionably neuromorphic."

Jake noticed a WC insignia on the corner of the chip—the one Winston always carried in his pocket.

"Wait a minute," said Winston, "that's my chip! I must have left it in the pocket of my old shirt—the one that I changed in a quick visit to the USC lab two days ago. How stupid of me!"

Jake quickly recalled Winston's threat that "one day he would exact his revenge."

Jake thought in silence, Could it be possible that Winston was the murderer?

The President took control and said, "I want the CIA and the FBI branch in Utah on this case right away. Brian Orin lived in Salt Lake City and we have learned that Jet Stream Cleaning is headquartered in Utah."

"Pardon me, Mr. President," said Samantha. "I wouldn't do that because I believe the FBI office in Salt Lake City is tainted. But I do know one agent who can be trusted."

Chapter 42

LUPITA

L upita Luiz grew up in the whitest of the white Midwest; she knew all of the racial slurs: beaner, taco, brownie, and greaser among a litany of other racial slurs. She had, however, learned from her mother that bliss is just the ability to look beyond shortcomings.

Like her mother, Maria, Lupita Luiz always carried an apple corer. More than a good luck token, it served as a connection to her mother.

Lupita graduated from the Duke Law School at age twenty and, without hesitation, joined the Federal Bureau of Investigation. Becoming a member of the FBI was a dream since childhood. She was smarter than most and rapidly advanced through the ranks of the Bureau.

Nevertheless, it was just her luck to be assigned to the Salt Lake City office—not exactly Vahalla for a young female Latino. As in her youth, when her back was turned in the Bureau office, she would hear the same classic racial slurs. Thankfully, however, she partnered with Jack Wells. Jack was a veteran agent and became convinced that Lupita was a solid bureau agent. She was intelligent, industrious to a fault, and when necessary she could be as hard as nails. She was much like his wife, Sandra.

When Jack heard the whispers behind Lupita's back, he looked into her brown, sullen eyes and would tell her, "Screw them. They're just a bunch of racist assholes. You can bet, though, that each of them will be in temple on Sunday professing their righteousness."

Jack was surprised when his cell phone rang and the caller was identified as Samantha James. He didn't get a chance to even say hello. Samantha was breathing quickly and talking even faster.

"Jack, we are going to need your help," Samantha pleaded. "The senior senator from Utah, Brian Orin, has murdered the vice president and two well-known congressmen. When can you get to DC?"

Without hesitation, Jack responded, "My associate, Lupita Luiz, and I will take the red-eye out. We'll be there first thing in the morning."

Samantha was stunned. This can't be a coincidence, she pondered. *It must be my baby doll Lupita. I hope her mother is watching over her carefully.* Samantha found herself praying for Lupita's safekeeping.

As Jack and Lupita were briefed, it was all too evident that Winston Kelly was the primary suspect. Jack and Lupita interviewed Winston in a small office inside the Capitol. Winston elected not to engage legal counsel for he claimed he had nothing to hide.

Maybe he has nothing to hide, thought Jack, *but he was sweating bullets even before the interview began.*

Jack and Lupita carefully hurled a myriad of questions at Winston, ranging from his school days at Corona del Mar High School, to his studies at USC, to his involvement with his life partner, Charles Wertz, Project Artichoke, and the eventual development of the neuromorphic chip. Winston broke down as Jack brought up Charlie's death.

"You and your people led to his death," said Winston, "I was angry then and I'm still angry now."

"Angry enough to cause the death of three innocent people?" Jack inquired.

"Believe me, I thought long and hard about revenge, said Winston, "but murder is not one of my core values."

It was difficult to tell if Winston's tears were initiated by anger or the loss of his lover.

After two hours of questioning, Lupita heard a voice resonating in her head. The soft female voice said, "He is not the one."

Terrified, Lupita stood up and asked to speak with Jack outside the office.

"Jack," said Lupita, "he is not our target."

"How do you know?" asked Jack.

"Believe me, Jack," said Lupita, "I just know. He was not involved in these murders."

Jack replied, "I have been involved in hundreds of interviews and depositions in my career. I knew ten minutes into the interview that he was innocent, but I needed to obtain as much information from him as possible. What tipped you off, Lupita?" asked Jack.

"His asserted guilt was just too simple. The simplest route doesn't necessarily lead you to the truth," added Lupita.

"Nevertheless," said Jack, "for someone so young to have the ability to see through a witness so quickly is pretty surprising."

"Just lucky, I guess," said Lupita. Lupita did not tell Jack about the voice.

When they returned to the room housing Winston, he was still sobbing.

"All right, Mr. Kelly," said Jack, "you can go now. But keep us posted as to your location. Remember, you're still a suspect."

"Oh, don't worry," said Winston, "I'll be available. I'm as interested as you are to find out who is trying to implicate me in this matter."

Lupita was dreaming that night when she heard that voice again, "Don't be frightened—it's just me, your mother."

Lupita fell back to sleep and decided that she could cancel the appointment she had made with a local psychiatrist earlier in the day.

Chapter 43

MOTHER AND SON

⌒〜⌒

Jack turned to Lupita and said, "Let's circle back around and look into Jet Stream Cleaning. The corporate headquarters are close and located in the Zion Bank bordering on Joseph Smith Boulevard."

As Jack and Lupita entered the corporate offices, they had expected more. It was a small, dingy office occupied by two bookkeeping types and a receptionist that had watermelon-sized breasts. Jack and Lupita displayed their identification and asked for the owner, Abu Saleh al-Obaid.

The receptionist apprehensively responded, "Mr. al-Obaid has been dead for over two years. This office is merely a corporate shell that provides accounting, scheduling, and administrative functions. Jet Stream's principal operations are located in Los Angeles near the USC campus."

"Who is the current owner?" Jack asked the receptionist.

The receptionist quickly responded, "The new owner is Ayam al Zawahir, Mr. al-Obaid's nephew. At least, he is the one that signs our payroll checks. Ayam has recently changed his name to Evan Wakefield. We rarely see Mr. Wakefield, for his principal job is to service our largest client, the University of Southern California. Evan is a pleasing man and an exact opposite of his uncle."

"What do you mean by that?" said Jack.

The receptionist continued, "Mr. al-Obaid was a very difficult man to work for. He had a terrible temper and even worse, we could sense that he rarely bathed. When he came into the office, his odor permeated everything, even our clothing. My dry-cleaning bills were astronomical."

The bookkeeper-types in the back of the office were terrified by the presence of Jack and Lupita. They were hunched over their computers below a black standard on the wall that read in bold letters:

THE ISLAMIC STATE OF IRAN AND SYRIA

Jack looked into the eyes of the three employees and shouted, "Are any of you connected with ISIS?"

"Oh no, exclaimed the receptionist. "That black placard belonged to Mr. al-Obaid. We were instructed by Mr. al-Obaid, in no uncertain terms, to never remove it from the wall.

Although Mr. al-Obaid is dead, his dreadful temper continues to prevail. No one has the courage to remove the standard."

As they left the office, Jack turned to Lupita and said, "Get a couple of junior agents out here to question the people in this office. The last thing we need is to have ISIS in possession of a neuromorphic chip."

When Jack and Lupita returned to the Bureau office, she immediately ran a check on Ayam al Zawahir aka Evan Wakefield. The check was blocked and read "For Eyes of the US Department of Justice only."

Jack was pissed.

***

Saudi Arabia is a country in Western Asia comprised of approximately 830 thousand square miles and is the second largest state in the Arab world. It emerged into the modern-day country sometime in the early seventh century when Mohammed united the population and created a universal religious doctrine.

Saudi Arabia has the largest economy in the Middle East, in light of its significant petroleum reserves and production. Nearly half of the country's 35 million people are under the age of 25.

But despite a liberal and youthful population, there continues to be a strict observance of moral and social behavior and those that go outside the guidelines are often subjected to brutal capital punishment orchestrated by religious leaders and jurists.

Ayam al Zawahir grew up in a Muslim family on a wheat farm just outside of Hejaz. He recalled little of his early childhood. He remembered running through the lush wheat fields, the constant fighting amongst his mother and father, and **that** particular night.

Gone were the days when every female was required to have a male guardian and was considered weak because they had no one to protect them. Ayam's mother, Pankaji, was strong and of the new breed that demanded respect from their husbands.

Respect was not a consideration in his parent's marriage, for Ayam's father was an anachronism—he felt that women were to be reined in and to be submissive to every wish and desire of their male counterparts.

Ayam's father was also an underground member of ISIS. Ayam could remember his father ranting about the United States. He called the US a land of infidels who did not comply with the interpretations of Islam and, as a result, it was proper to engage in violent actions against these infidels—even if innocents were killed. If one were to strike the infidels, it was likely that he or she would be called to Paradise.

Ayam was conflicted. His mother had secretly given him

an iPad and this access to social media provided him with a glamorous picture of the US and its population of infidels. Ayam didn't dare reveal these glamorous pictures to his father.

Most of all, Ayam remembered **that** night when he was awakened by the terrifying screams of his mother. Ayam flew from his bed and found his father violently choking Pankaji.

Ayam screamed, "Stop! You're killing her!!"

His father turned to him, displaying a demonic smile on his face. Ayam ran to the kitchen, seeking a butcher knife. When he returned to the struggle, he found that his mother was blue in the face and barely breathing.

Ayam screamed again, but now in a more forceful tone, "Stop or I will kill you!!"

Ayam didn't wait. He forced the blade through his father's back until it penetrated deep into his flaccid flesh. He then removed the knife and stabbed over and over again until his father released his grip on Pankaji's throat.

Ayam caressed his sobbing mother until she could breathe once again.

"I am sorry, mother. He was about to kill you," exclaimed Ayam.

"Don't worry," said Pankaji, "Please get my cell phone—it's on the top of my dresser."

She quickly dialed the confidential number—it turned out

it was the phone number of Nole Pacis at the US Department of Justice.

Nole answered his cell and in a hushed tone said, "Hello, Pankaji, this is not our designated time to speak. What's wrong? Are you in a safe space?" he asked.

"Mr. Pacis, I am in a safe space right now, but I fear it will not be safe for long. I have killed my husband," said Pankaji. "I have been of great assistance to you and your department throughout the years. Now I desperately need your help. My son and I need to leave Saudi Arabia immediately!"

Without reservation, Nole responded "I can get a US government plane from Turkey to the King Abdulaziz Airport in four hours." Nole continued, "I will have some of my people at your home within the hour. They will tidy things up to give the impression that there was a break-in and that you and your son have been kidnapped. A ransom note to your father will be left behind.

"Pankaji, you have always been very careful," said Nole. "But now it is extremely important that there is no evidence that can link you with the US Department of Justice. We don't need to create an international incident."

"I understand," said Pankaji. "There will be no such evidence."

"You are an important package," said Nole. "I'll make sure

you connect with your brother in Salt Lake City. I'm sure it's no surprise to you, but your brother is on the Bureau's watch list. If you ever need help while in Salt Lake City, please call Jack Wells at Salt Lake City FBI. He is a close friend."

Pankaji and Ayam thankfully, never saw Saudi Arabia again.

Chapter 44

MURDER IN THE LAB

Evan Wakefield was cleaning Winston's lab late Thursday night when his cell phone rang. It was Mohammed, his brother-in-law and best friend. Evan Wakefield decided to sit down and casually smoke a Marlboro Light.

Mohammed was a somewhat renowned computer analyst and a full professor at the University of Tennessee. It was 3:00 a.m. in Tennessee. Mohammed rarely slept.

Mohammed was the first to speak. "Evan, what is this chip you sent to me?"

Evan quickly responded, "As you know, I clean the offices of Winston Kelly and Charles Wertz. I'm sure you have heard of them."

"Of course," said Mohammed. "Perhaps the greatest computer theorists in the world. I was sorry to hear of Mr. Wertz's death. Nevertheless, it doesn't explain the chip."

"After cleaning the lab office last week," continued Mohammed, "I emptied my vacuum bag and noticed a small, glossy piece of metal amidst the dust. I am certainly no engineer, but it appeared to be some form of microchip. A week later, I found another chip in my vacuum bag."

"Ever since I found these microchips, I have been surrounded by a powerful sense of fear. Winston and Charlie were my friends and they would often speak openly before me, albeit it was in hushed tones. They often spoke of a special chip and its dangerous implications."

"Then Charlie committed suicide and now Winston is missing. I also sense that someone is following me. Mohammed, I have to tell you this entire set of circumstances is scaring the crap out of me."

Mohammed appealed to Evan asking him to calm down. "I wouldn't worry. It's probably just a set of coincidences that are toying with your imagination. You said you found two chips— what happened to the other one?"

"I spoke of my fears with my mother. She frantically urged me to send both of the chips to Nole Pacis at the Department of Justice. I sent the first to Mr. Pacis and for no other reason other than instinct, I sent the recently discovered chip to you. I suppose my overactive imagination thought you would be able to negotiate a bargain if my life was in jeopardy. I guess I sound like a small child that is deathly afraid of the monsters in a dark bedroom."

"Hold on," said Evan. "Someone is knocking at the door."

Evan set the cell phone on Winston's desk.

He opened the lab door to find two men in dark suits with guns in hand.

"Are you Evan Wakefield?" asked one of the intruders.

"Yes," Evan responded.

"My name is Agent Matthews and this is my associate Agent Zarrilli."

The intruders quickly used nylon ties to bind Evans's hands.

Evan offered no resistance, but said, "What is this all about?"

Matthews told Evan to sit on the floor.

"We would just like to ask you a couple of questions," said Matthews.

Evan began to panic and he could feel the urine quickly soaking his Jet Stream uniform. Evan turned to the intruders and said, "I am a nationalized US citizen and have done nothing wrong. What do you want of me?"

Matthews disregarded Evans's plea and tendered a question of his own.

"We know you found at least one electronic chip in this office recently and sent it to the Department of Justice. Is this correct?"

"Yes," said Evan. "I sent it directly to Nole Pacis."

Matthews pressed further. "Is that the only chip you discovered?"

Evan stuttered and was sweating profusely.

"Be very careful, Mr. Wakefield, you could be in grave danger if you don't provide us with the truth," said Matthews.

Evan stuttered again and said, "I found another chip and sent it to my brother-in-law."

"What is his name and where can we find him," responded Matthews.

Evan said, "His name is Mohammed al-Deza and he teaches computer science at the University of Tennessee. Please assure me that no harm will come to him."

Matthews was unrelenting. "Are you sure you found only two chips?"

"I am positive," said Evan.

"This interview is concluded," Matthews said sharply. "Zarrilli, do your job."

Zarrilli, in a perfect execution mode, placed his pistol at the back of Evan's head and pulled the trigger. Just to be sure, Zarrilli put two more bullets in Evan's head before he hit the ground. Zarrilli then picked up two of the shell casings; one slipped under the desk.

Mohammed had heard everything, including the shots. He

was shaking uncontrollably but he was able to call the LA Police Department and Evan's mother, Pankaji.

Mohammed remembered his uncle ranting that it is the duty of Muslims to exert as much force as possible to terrorize the enemies of God.

Chapter 45

FIRE

Pankaji received the call from Mohammed. She screamed in terror, "Oh no, not my baby!"

Without hesitation, Pankaji called Nole Pacis's friend, Jack Wells, at the Salt Lake City FBI Bureau. She quickly introduced herself and explained her relationship with Nole Pacis in between her roaring tears.

"Calm down, Mrs. al-Obaid. Let me see what I can find out. I have a contact that was formerly an LA police officer," said Jack Wells.

Wells quickly called Stephen James.

"Mr. James, this is Jack Wells at the FBI. I need a favor. I wonder if you could snoop around a murder scene at Winston Kelly's office on the USC campus. It's possible that this murder could be a matter of national security."

Stephen replied, "I still have friends in the department, but there are no guarantees that they'll let me observe the crime scene. I'll do the best I can. Are Samantha and PJ ok?"

Jack replied, "I haven't heard from either of them for a while but you can be assured they are not involved in this murder. Just relax," said Jack.

Three hours later, Stephen returned Jack's call. "I didn't get a chance to spend a great deal of time in Winston's office, but there is no question that it was a professional job. I don't know how you want to file this, but I found a shell casing from the new CIA pistol."

Jack raised his voice to say, "That damned Pacis is involved in this."

Jack was about to pick up the phone and call Mrs. al-Obaid when he was handed a large envelope. It was a return receipt parcel and clearly marked personal and confidential. He opened the envelope to find the Mullen committee report that was to be presented before Congress. The draft was entitled, *The Inherent Dangers Associated with the Neuromorphic Chip.*

Jack sat down and rapidly read through the report.

When he finished reading the committee report, he bolted from his chair trying to assimilate the death of Evan Wakefield and the Mullen committee members. He wondered if there was even a remote connection.

Lupita pulled Jack aside and told him that Nole Pacis was on the phone. "He says it's urgent," she stated.

"It had better be," said Jack. "Nole, you bastard," Jack

snarled. Jack went silent as he carefully listened to Nole. Jack's eyes widened.

As soon as he hung up from Nole, Jack turned to Lupita and said, "Call Samantha and her group and tell them to meet us at the Oakridge National Laboratory in Tennessee."

Lupita asked, "Why Oakridge?"

"It's the home of the US supercomputers," Jack said quickly.

Lupita was confused.

***

Nole Pacis and the President sat in a dark hotel room, just outside of the Capitol. Nole's men had thoroughly searched the room to ensure that it was absent of any bugs or listening devices.

The President was clearly remorseful when he said to Nole, "Those were four damn fine people."

"Mr. President, we simply had no choice at that point," said Nole. "Orin and Mullen insisted on releasing the committee report."

"Initially, they would have revealed the existence of neuromorphic chips," explained Nole. "That, in itself, would be a shock. More importantly, they would have proposed that if such a chip was introduced into one of our supercomputers, it was likely to infect other computers. Within days this artificial intelligence could shut down every communication and power source in the world. Suddenly, we would be at the bottom of the food chain and on the brink of anarchy. "Unfortunately, we have now discovered that the lives of Orin and the Mullen committee members were needlessly wasted."

Nole continued, "One of the chips was sent to me and implanted into Orin. I thought our problem would be temporarily abated and we would have a window to solve this issue of an artificial intelligence.

"We have now discovered, however, that Evan Wakefield subsequently found another chip and sent it to his brother-in-law. The brother-in-law is a respected computer analyst and a professor at the University of Tennessee. It's possible that he may also have a remote association with ISIS and may have access to a supercomputer. If he does have access, he might be able to implant the chip and its potential artificial intelligence capabilities into the supercomputer," Nole added.

"Not exactly the basis for a jubilant outcome," said the President. "It's not likely that we can destroy every computer in the world."

"Hardly, Mr. President," said Pacis.

"Jack Wells somehow got a copy of the Mullen committee report," said Nole. "Jack is a hardassed FBI agent and he's smart enough to realize the implications of singularity. I have asked him to take his team of specialists to Oakridge to see if our supers have been contaminated, and if so, if is there a means to unwind the artificial intelligence implant. I would suggest, Mr. President, that you take the elevator to the underground safe place," urged Pacis.

***

Jack bullied Samantha, her son, Winston, and Jake into the sterile room that housed the supercomputers mainframe at Oakridge.

Winston and PJ commenced their data entry countdown to see if that computer had, through transmission, been infected.

Within ten minutes, Winston turned to PJ and said, "We're screwed! It's been breached and the breach looks like it has extended its aggressive infection to every supercomputer that we know of."

PJ snapped at Winston, "Remember that Nelson Mandela once commented that things are always impossible until they are done? I suggest that we take a chance and try to reach the power nine processor. The processor might allow us to reverse the effects of the artificial intelligence."

"It's a reach," said Winston. "It could also be very dangerous if the computer has implemented a fail-safe device. Nevertheless, it's a good idea, PJ. I don't think we have any other choice."

Jake suddenly felt a strong bond to Samantha, gripped her hand, and whispered in her ear, "I probably have waited too long to tell you that I love you."

Samantha smiled softly. She hoped it wasn't too late.

Winston went to the memory petabytes in the board searching for the processor. He was sweating profuscly and after two hours, he screamed, "I found the processor and next to it the neuromorphic chip. Jake, come and look at this." With a touch of the exit panel, Winston said, "I think I…"

Winston wasn't able to complete his sentence, for an electric arc leapt from the computer and consumed him in a fiery blaze.

PJ then screamed, "The computer does have a failsafe device! Get the hell out of here!"

Suddenly the entire room was set ablaze and, in the commotion, only Samantha, PJ, and Lupita could reach the fireproof door. Jake was lost.

Out of the flames, PJ caressed his mother and Lupita.

"What next?" asked Samantha.

"We have one remaining alternative," said PJ. "I would suggest we pray."

"Please, Lord God, just one more time," Samantha whispered.

Chapter 46

THE SISTERS IN MOURNING

Each of the sisters had tears in her eyes.

The Lord God said to Her sister Maria, "We must do the best we can but our children are enveloped by a network of computers that will eventually lead to their ultimate demise."

"Lord God, I fear you may be blinded by a fear of doom; perhaps you should rely on your sight alone," said Maria.

"You are right, Maria," said the Lord God, "but I feel that our options are limited."

"I know I am wallowing in self-pity but if we fail it will be the fourth time we have lost all of our children on this planet earth."

"Should we try one more time, perhaps? Maria, you should begin to create a fifth Eve. I will embark on creating a new Garden of Eden."

In a sobbing voice, Maria said, "And what of Adam?"

The Lord God replied, "Right now, I'm not necessarily

convinced about introducing a fifth Adam. The male species is often more trouble than they are worth. We'll talk about this later."

The Sisters turned to face each other as they heard the faint prayers of Samantha, PJ, and Lupita.

* * *

Two millenniums later, the Lord God and Maria were tending the apple grove once owned by Samantha, James, and PJ. It was a somber time when the human race was about to self-destruct for the fifth time.

The Lord God turned to Maria and reminded her that they were the Presence and had the prerogative to collapse the universe or expand it and have it continue in perpetuity.

The Lord God said to Maria, "I am not a quitter but I tire of this small planet; as long as there is free will there will be a course of action that leads to destruction."

Maria nodded her head in agreement.

As the sisters walked from the grove there was a great deal of regret and tears, The farther that they walked from the grove it became darker and darker. Suddenly there was an end to all that existed.

ABOUT THE AUTHOR

Stephen L. Newman graduated from the University of Southern California with Magna Cum Laude honors. As a Certified Public Accountant, Mr. Newman initially represented talent and production entities in a number of major motion pictures.

More recently, he has concentrated on representing foreign interests and US citizens in significant controversies with various tax authorities.

Mr. Newman has been married for 52 years, has 5 children and 7 grandchildren. He and his wife reside in Orange County, California.

Made in the USA
Middletown, DE
19 February 2022

61238559R00139